More Tales from the Ark

Avril Rowlands

Illustrations by Rosslyn Moran

A LION BOOK

D1470853

Text copyright © 1995 Avril Rowlands
Illustrations copyright © 1995 Rosslyn Moran

The author asserts the moral right
to be identified as the author of this work

Published by
Lion Publishing plc
Sandy Lane West, Oxford, England
ISBN 0 7459 3035 2
Albatross Books Pty Ltd
PO Box 320, Sutherland, NSW 2232, Australia
ISBN 0 7324 1257 9

First edition 1995
10 9 8 7 6 5 4 3

A catalogue record for this book is available
from the British Library

Printed and bound in Great Britain
by Cox & Wyman Ltd, Reading

CONTENTS

1
NOAH'S TALE

Mr Noah was a worried man. He had been ever since God had dropped his bombshell and turned Mr Noah's life upside down.

'I am afraid,' God had said to Mr Noah, 'that I shall have to destroy the world and every living creature, for it has become an evil place. But I shall save you, Mr Noah, and your wife and sons and their wives. And I shall save two of all the living creatures in the world.'

God told Mr Noah to build a wooden ark, which was like a large boat, so that when he sent a flood to cover the earth, Mr Noah, his family and the animals would be saved.

'And you, Mr Noah, will look after the animals for me, for they are all important. I'm relying on you to keep them alive.'

Mr Noah was sad at the thought of the world being destroyed and worried at the job God had given him to do. He pleaded with God.

'I'm very grateful, God, please believe me, but I don't think I'm the right person. I've never kept any animals apart from two cats, and I've only got them to keep the mice down. I don't even really like animals. I'm sure you could choose someone better than me.'

But God wanted Mr Noah.

Mr Noah tried again. 'I'm not a very good organizer, God, and you'll need a good organizer for this trip. I get muddled, you see.'

But God did not reply. Besides, he had every faith in Mr Noah.

'It's not as if I'm a young man,' Mr Noah told his wife that night. 'God should have chosen a younger, better man for the job.' (Mr Noah was six hundred years old at the time.)

'A younger one maybe,' said his wife, 'but there's not a better one. And God chose *you* for the job, so do try and get some sleep.'

But sleep would not come to Mr Noah that night. He tossed and turned and worried. At last he sat bolt upright.

'What on earth do aardvarks eat?' he demanded. But his wife was snoring gently by his side and did not reply.

Mr Noah had had little sleep since then. As the days passed, his worries grew.

'Ouch!' he cried, as he hit his thumb with a hammer for the third time.

'Look, Father,' said his eldest son Shem, 'why don't

you go and welcome the animals and leave building the ark to us?'

His other sons, Ham and Japheth, nodded in agreement.

'I'm sure you've plenty of other work to do,' Shem added tactfully.

'And you know you're not much good at carpentry,' Ham said bluntly.

Mr Noah looked stubborn. 'God told *me* to build the ark,' he said.

Shem, Ham and Japheth looked at each other, then carried on with the building. But after a few minutes ...

'Owwh!' cried Mr Noah, as he hit his sore thumb for a fourth time.

'Please, Father ...' said Shem.

Just then Mrs Noah called from the house.

'Noah, will you come? Two flamingos have arrived and say they must speak to you. They seem a bit upset.'

Mr Noah climbed down from the ark. He was really quite pleased to have an excuse to go, and his sons were equally pleased to be rid of him.

'Now we can get on faster,' said Ham.

Mr Noah did not return to the ark. After he had talked to the flamingos, the chimpanzees had to be chased off his grapevines. Then the beavers arrived and began building a dam across the stream which provided water for Mr Noah's farm. The emus turned their noses up at

the sleeping arrangements and one of the polar bears fainted with the heat. Mr Noah was kept very busy. There was so much to do and so little time.

'Can't you get some of the animals to give you a hand?' his wife asked, as they ate their evening meal. 'Those nice elephants offered to help the boys with the building, and even the monkeys said they'd swing down and pick up the tools that got dropped—not that I trust them that much. Very sarcastic they were.'

'The beavers want to help, too,' said Japheth.

'I can't have help,' Mr Noah replied. 'God gave *me* the job and I must do it by myself.'

'But you're not building the ark by yourself,' his wife pointed out. 'Our sons are helping.'

'Yes,' said Mr Noah, frowning. 'But perhaps I should have tried.'

'The ark would sink,' Ham said.

'Don't be so rude to your father!' said his mother sharply, but Mr Noah was not even listening.

How could he make sure that two of every animal, insect, and bird were on board at the right time? Say he missed one or two? God might never forgive him. Word must already have got around, for animals were beginning to arrive, turning up at Mr Noah's farmhouse at all hours of the day and night. It was a problem knowing where to put them and how to feed them, and the two chimpanzees could not be stopped from stripping the grapes from his vineyards.

Food was another problem. How was he to get all the food required for so many animals? Mr Noah spent hours making lists of what the animals, insects and birds ate. It made depressing reading, for many of them just ate each other.

Then there was the building of the ark itself, which kept being held up as Mr Noah was too busy to supervise the work.

Worries piled up along with the lists in Mr Noah's office. He grew short-tempered and his sons and their wives and even Mrs Noah began to avoid him. And as the day for boarding the ark drew nearer, Mr Noah began to panic.

'It'll never be ready on time,' he thought, and hit his thumbs and fingers as he tried to work faster.

'The food'll never arrive in time,' he thought, and sent out messages far and wide.

And one dreadful afternoon when the beavers successfully dammed his stream and all the water to his farm dried up, and his vineyards—long since stripped of grapes—were finally trampled down by the hippos and the elephants, Mr Noah despaired.

He stopped doing any work and sat in the wreckage of his once beautiful farm. Sadly he thought of his past life, remembering how he had enjoyed watching his grapes grow round and fat under the summer sun. Although he had complained about the hard work, he had been content with his life. His eyes misted over and two fat tears fell on the long list he held in his hand. He was too old for change and it was all very frightening.

'I can't do it,' he thought, as he caught sight of the chimpanzees scratching themselves for fleas. 'Should two fleas be taken on the ark?' he wondered. God had not said anything about fleas.

He put his head in his hands and groaned. 'I can't do it.'

Then he jumped to his feet and began to pace up and down.

'I can't, I *can't*, I CAN'T DO IT! God will have to find someone else. It's not too late.'

'Noah.'

It was God speaking, but Mr Noah did not hear him at first; he was too upset.

'Noah, listen to me.'

'Oh, God, is that you?' Mr Noah said, words falling over themselves in his panic. 'Where have you been? I've been so upset and so worried and got into such a state.

13

I don't want to leave, I can't leave, and I can't do the job you've given me. I don't want to die in the flood, but this is too much for an old man. Anyway, I don't like animals—you should see the way some of them behave! Please, God, find someone else.'

'Noah,' said God patiently. 'Stop talking, sit down and be quiet for a moment.'

Mr Noah did what God said and immediately began to feel a bit better.

'Now then, are you listening?'

'Yes, God,' said Mr Noah.

'Good. I've been wanting to help you for a long time, but you haven't given me the chance.'

'Haven't I?'

'No. You've been too busy trying to do everything yourself.'

'Have I?'

'Yes.'

'Oh,' said Mr Noah. 'I thought that was what you wanted.'

'You should have asked me, Noah,' said God.

'You haven't been around much lately,' Mr Noah grumbled. Then he felt ashamed. 'I expect you've been too busy.'

'I'm never too busy to help you,' said God. 'As long as you trust me, everything will turn out well.'

'Yes, God,' said Mr Noah.

'*Do* you trust me?' God asked, and it seemed to Mr Noah, as he sat in the sun among his ruined vineyards, that this was the most important question he had ever been asked. He thought back over his long life, remembering how, even as a child, he had always taken his problems to God. And God had never let him down, he thought. Not once. It was a long time before he spoke.

'Yes,' he said at last. 'Yes, God, I do trust you.'

'Well then,' said God. 'There's nothing for you to worry about.'

Mr Noah sat for a while longer, enjoying a sense of peace he had not known for a long time. Then he went back to his house and told his wife and sons that he was sorry for having been so bad-tempered. Everyone felt so much better that they worked even harder. Some of the animals helped, and soon the ark was ready.

And if Mr Noah still had worries, which he had—especially when he saw some of the more ferocious animals arrive on his farm—and if his stomach felt churned up at the thought of the future, which it did—many times a day—no one knew about it, except God. And God, Mr Noah knew, would help him with whatever lay ahead.

2
THE PEACOCK'S TALE

Once the ark had been built, Mr Noah and his sons filled it with food, water and everything that might possibly be needed for the long voyage ahead. For God had told Mr Noah that he would send a great flood to cover the earth, but that Mr Noah, his family, and two of every animal, insect and bird would be kept safe inside the ark.

Mr Noah packed some things for himself and put on his second-best robe.

'There's no point taking our *best* clothes,' he said to his wife, 'as there'll be plenty of dirty jobs to do on the ark. I don't think many of the animals will be house-trained.'

'Well, I'm not leaving my best robe to be ruined in the flood!' Mrs Noah retorted, and put it on.

Mr Noah walked slowly round his farm for the very last time before pinning a large notice to the front door:

GONE AWAY. ENQUIRIES TO THE ARK.
ADDRESS UNKNOWN.

'There's no point locking the place up,' he thought sadly.

But Mr Noah did not have time for any more sad thoughts. He was kept far too busy standing at the entrance to the ark, welcoming the animals, insects and birds and ticking them off on a great long list. Mrs Noah stood beside him dressed in her best robe, and very fine she looked too.

When everyone was safely inside, God himself shut the door behind them.

Some of the animals settled in quickly, grateful for shelter from the storm clouds gathering overhead. But one or two were full of complaints. The peacock was the worst.

'It really isn't good enough,' he said, strutting up and down the great hall, his beak turned up at the noise and smell of the other animals.

'Never mind, dear,' said his wife, a rather drab-looking little peahen.

'What isn't good enough?' asked the fox, who was eyeing the two dormice with mouth-watering interest.

'Any of this,' said the peacock, fanning out his beautiful tail. 'I never thought that my beloved wife and I would be required to *share* accommodation on this voyage. I shall have to complain.'

'Who to?' asked the fox. 'God? I think he's *far* too busy right now to attend to you.' He chuckled at the

thought, much to the relief of the dormice, who hurriedly scuttled away.

'To "The Management",' the peacock replied grandly.

'What's that?' asked the buffalo, blowing water out through his nose. The peacock looked at him in disgust.

' "The Management", I imagine, is that shabbily-dressed person who welcomed us on board. If it could be called a welcome,' he went on. 'I did not like having to wait in a queue with the rabble.'

'Who is the rabble?' asked the donkey. 'I don't think I've heard of an animal of that name, but then there are so many wonderful creatures here I've never heard of. It's been quite an eye-opener for me.'

'Huh!' snorted the peacock, and stalked off in search of Mr Noah. His wife hurried after him.

'Silly old thing,' said the buffalo. 'Just who does he think he is?'

'It's his wife I feel sorry for,' said the rabbit comfortably. 'I wouldn't like to be married to him.'

The peacock found Mr Noah in his cabin, putting the finishing touches to a large notice:

RULES OF THE ARK
1. PASSENGERS ARE REQUESTED NOT TO FIGHT
2. PASSENGERS ARE ABSOLUTELY FORBIDDEN
   TO EAT EACH OTHER DURING THE VOYAGE
3. ANY COMPLAINTS ARE TO BE REFERRED TO ME
   OR MY ASSISTANTS, LION AND TIGER

Mr Noah

Mr Noah looked up as the peacock and peahen entered. 'Hello. What can I do for you?'

'I've a complaint,' said the peacock.

'Oh dear,' said Mr Noah. He sat on his bed. 'How can I help?'

'I'm sure you'll agree that my tail is very beautiful,' the peacock began, unfurling it in the small cabin and smudging Mr Noah's notice in the process.

'Yes, indeed,' said Mr Noah.

'I would say,' said the peacock, 'that I have a more beautiful tail than any other creature in the world.'

'Very possibly,' said Mr Noah.

'It's a great responsibility,' the peacock went on, 'and I have to spend a lot of time looking after it.'

'I'm sure,' Mr Noah said in a respectful voice.

'I need peace, quiet and space for this,' the peacock went on. 'And there's neither peace, quiet or space in the great hall.'

'No,' said Mr Noah. 'I don't suppose there is.'

'Mr Noah, I am a sensitive and highly-strung bird. I don't ask for much. Just a cabin to myself—with my dear wife of course...' He looked disdainfully around Mr Noah's cabin. '... A little larger than this would suit me perfectly. And meals to be served in my room. I really *cannot* be expected to eat with the other animals.'

Mr Noah sighed. 'I'm very sorry but I can't do that. We haven't any spare cabins at all. There's an awful lot of animals, insects and birds to be accommodated.'

'But that's not good enough...' the peacock began, his voice getting louder.

'Well, God designed the ark,' said Mr Noah, 'and he's very economical. He never wastes anything he's created. I'm afraid that there's nothing at all I can do.'

'I see,' snapped the peacock, and he stormed out of the cabin.

'Now, dear, don't take on so,' said his wife as she

hurried after him. 'It'll only give you a funny turn. You know it will.'

Mr Noah sighed again. 'Oh dear, God,' he said. 'Whatever am I to do? As if I hadn't enough problems already.'

'This one will go away,' said God. 'You'll see.'

But the problem did not go away. In fact, it got worse. The peacock complained all day and every day and soon many of the other animals started complaining too. The giraffes demanded more headroom, the hippos more water, the penguins more ice, the bats more dark and the butterflies more light.

'There ought to have been different *classes* of accommodation,' said the emu self-righteously.

'Based on what?' asked the buffalo. 'The length of your tail?'

'I wouldn't stand a chance then,' said the guinea-pig cheerfully. ' 'Cause I haven't got one.'

'And I'd get chucked out of first class,' said the gecko. 'For mine's just dropped off.'

'What do you mean?' asked the donkey, quite mystified.

The gecko shrugged. 'My tail always drops off if I get a fright.'

'What gave you a fright?' asked the rhinoceros.

'Your ugly face for a start,' said the gecko, and slithered off, laughing.

'Those lizards,' sniffed the emu. '*Very* underbred.' And she went to find the peacock, who was holding forth at the far end of the hall.

'I feel that God should have been more selective,' the peacock was saying as the emu joined him. 'Why decide to save two of every animal, insect and bird in creation, when we all know there are plenty we could happily do without?'

'You for one,' the swallow called down from her perch.

'It would have been a wonderful opportunity for God to have tidied things up a bit,' the peacock went on. 'If some of the rougher, uglier animals had not been allowed on the ark, there would have been more room for the rest of us.' He pulled his tail away from the jackdaw who had just flown in and perched on it.

The animals began to grow tired of the peacock's grumbles and more and more of them complained to Mr Noah.

'I wouldn't mind if he'd only talk a little more quietly,' said the ostrich. 'But he's got such a loud, unpleasant voice it's given me quite a headache.'

There were so many complaints that Mr Noah locked himself in his cabin and refused to hear any more.

'What *am* I to do, God?' he asked.

'Don't worry,' said God, 'and do nothing.'

'I can't help but worry,' Mr Noah said crossly, but he

took God's advice and did nothing.

The next day the peacock did not appear in the great hall, much to the relief of many of the animals.

'Probably giving his boring old tail a spring-clean,' said the guinea-pig.

'I wish it would fall out,' said the otter. 'I'm that fed up with him going on about it.'

'But it's so beautiful,' sighed the donkey. 'I wish mine was half as beautiful.'

'If only he was as beautiful *inside* as he is *outside*,' said the buffalo. 'I know I'm ugly, but at least I'm not vain.'

The following day the peacock was still missing. The peahen was missing too. On the third day Mr Noah began a search, but it was some time before he discovered them, hidden away in the darkest corner of the ark. The peacock was sobbing.

'It's the most awful thing that's ever happened!'

'Now then, what's the trouble?' said Mr Noah.

The peahen turned to him. 'Oh dear, Mr Noah, he'll die from the shame of it.'

'Whatever's wrong?' asked Mr Noah.

The peacock came out from the corner in which he was hiding and Mr Noah gasped. For every one of his beautiful tail feathers had gone.

'Bald,' sobbed the peacock. 'Tail-less. I can't, I just can't face them!'

'How did it happen?' Mr Noah asked.

'All peacocks lose their tails,' said the peahen. 'I told him so, but he wouldn't listen. He never listens to me. Perhaps it'll teach the silly thing a lesson,' she added tartly, while the peacock sobbed even louder.

It look a lot of persuading before the peacock would agree to follow Mr Noah into the great hall. His arrival caused uproar.

The jackdaw fell off his perch laughing, while the buffalo spluttered so much that he nearly choked.

'Serves him right,' said the gecko, whose own tail was beginning to grow again.

'You don't rate even third-class accommodation,' said the rhinoceros bluntly. 'If God saw you now you wouldn't even get a place on the ark!'

'All right,' said the peacock in a tearful voice. 'I'm sorry. I thought I was better than all of you, because of my tail, but I'm not. I shouldn't have said the things I did. But it was a b-b-beautiful tail,' he added, beginning to sob again.

Just then the eagle called out in his great voice.

'Quiet, everyone!'

In the silence that followed they could all hear a heavy drumming noise on the roof of the ark.

'The rain has begun,' said the eagle. He spread his great wings.

'I think,' he said, 'that there should be no more complaints. There are more important things to worry about than the peacock's tail. If we had been left outside, we should all have perished.'

No one could disagree with that and the animals, insects and birds were unusually quiet as they went to their perches, nests and holes that night.

3

THE POLAR BEAR'S TALE

It had been raining for some days now and the ark was starting to float on a rising flood of water. It was very crowded on board, as two of every animal, insect and bird in creation take up a great deal of space, but gradually everyone began to settle down. Soon all the animals had, more or less, found a place for themselves and were, more or less, happy. Everyone, that is, apart from the polar bear.

For the polar bear, having come from a land where there were very few animals, was quite amazed by the number and variety he saw around him. He wanted to make friends with all of them, but did not know how to go about it. So he prowled around, making the smaller animals nervous and the larger ones puzzled.

'What's he after?' asked the rhinoceros suspiciously.

'I don't know that he's *after* anything,' said the brown bear.

The rhinoceros was not convinced. 'If he thinks he can wallow in my water, he's got another think coming.'

'I just want to be friends,' said the polar bear.

'Why?' asked the other rhinoceros.

The polar bear did not know how to answer that and ambled away. Making friends was not as easy as he had first thought. Then he had an idea. If he agreed with everything the animals said, they would be sure to like him.

'It's so cold here,' grumbled the camel. 'I feel it after the heat of the desert.'

'Yes, it is cold,' said the polar bear, who secretly thought the great hall was uncomfortably warm.

'It's not the cold,' said the cheetah, pacing restlessly up and down. 'It's the boredom. I want to feel the wind in my fur as I run through the wild country.'

'I'm bored too,' agreed the polar bear.

'Well I find all this rather restful,' said the tiger sleepily. 'Not having to find my food, not having any responsibilities. I could get used to this life.'

'So could I,' the polar bear agreed.

'I'll tell you what's *boring* around here,' snapped the rhinoceros crossly. 'Animals that agree with everything you say. That's what's *really* boring.'

'Yes,' said the polar bear. 'That's very true.'

The rhinoceros snorted and walked off, and one by one the other animals followed.

'Why do I always say the wrong thing?' the polar bear said later to his wife. 'I only want to be friends.'

'You try too hard,' his wife said. 'You should just be yourself.'

'But I want them to like me,' said the polar bear unhappily.

'You can't *make* people like you,' said his wife. 'You mustn't mind so much.'

But the polar bear did mind. He minded very much indeed. Every day he went into the great hall and tried to make friends with one or other of the animals. But the more he tried, the worse it became. The animals first made fun of him and then ignored him, so he took to sitting in the rain on the roof of the ark, quite alone and most unhappy.

'If I said I had two heads,' said the hippopotamus, 'you know what the polar bear would say?'

'What?' asked the giraffe.

'He'd say that he had two heads as well,' replied the hippo and burst into a gruff laugh.

'That's rather unkind,' said Mr Noah, who was passing at the time. 'He only wants to be friends.'

'I choose my friends,' said the camel haughtily. 'And I don't make friends with colourless animals who have no conversation and come from outlandish places.'

'He can't help his colour,' said Mr Noah mildly.

'Or lack of it,' said the lion, looking with pride at his great golden mane.

Mr Noah turned to the brown bear. 'Perhaps you'd be

his friend?' he said. 'After all, you are related.'

'Only distantly,' said the brown bear hurriedly. But the brown bear was a kind animal, so he padded off. He found the polar bear sitting in his usual place, hunched up on the roof of the ark.

'What are you doing all by yourself?' the brown bear asked, poking his head through the trap door. 'It's wet and miserable up here.'

'It's better by myself,' said the polar bear sadly. 'Then I don't upset the others. Oh, brown bear, you've got lots of friends. Tell me what I should do to make them like me.'

The brown bear thought about it for a while, then a slow smile began to spread across his face and he licked his lips.

'Just give them honey,' he said.

'Honey?' repeated the polar bear.

'Nothing like honey for making friends,' said the brown bear. 'Can't get enough of it myself.'

'Where do I get it from?' asked the polar bear.

'From bees, of course,' said the brown bear, shaking his head at such ignorance.

'Bees?'

The brown bear nodded. 'But don't tell them I told you. Funny things, bees. Temperamental. You want to be careful with bees.'

The polar bear took his advice and approached the bees very carefully.

'Excuse me,' he said politely.

The bees came out of their hive and buzzed round his head.

'Could I... is it possible...? Could I have some honey?' he asked.

'Honey?' they repeated.

'Please,' said the polar bear politely.

'You want honey?' asked the bees.

'If you don't mind,' said the polar bear.

'What do you want it for?' one of the bees asked suspiciously.

'To make friends,' said the polar bear. 'So that the other animals will like me.'

The bees buzzed together for some time. Then one of them turned to the polar bear.

'No,' she said. 'We don't give honey to polar bears.'

'Why not?' asked the polar bear, mystified.

'Because no polar bear has ever asked for any honey before,' said the other bee.

'But I'm asking you now,' said the polar bear.

'Sorry,' said the bee. And they both went into their hive and closed the door.

'Don't you worry,' said the brown bear when he heard about it later. 'I'll get it for you. Me and the bees are the best of friends.'

'Aren't you lucky,' said the polar bear enviously. 'I wish the bees would become *my* best friends.'

The brown bear went to the hive and knocked on the door, but the bees were out. He hesitated a moment, scratching his head.

'They won't miss a little honey if I take it,' he thought to himself. 'It's not really stealing as it's not for me.'

Reassured, he helped himself. But as he was carrying the honey away from the hive, the sweet smell of it made his nose twitch and his mouth water.

'What am I doing giving this honey to the polar bear?' he thought. 'He won't make any friends with it. Much better if *I* eat it. I can be his friend if he wants one.'

So he sat down and ate all the honey.

When the bees returned to their hive they were furious.

'It's that polar bear!' they said, buzzing furiously. 'Just wait till we get him!'

'It wasn't the polar bear,' said the skylark. 'He's still up on the roof. It was the brown bear.'

'Right,' said the bees, and they chased the brown bear round and round the ark until he grew quite dizzy.

'Leave me alone!' he squealed. 'I'm sorry . . . I won't do it again . . . !'

'That'll teach you to steal,' buzzed the bees angrily.

The animals thought it a very good joke and laughed at the brown bear. But it did not make them feel any more kindly towards the polar bear.

'Should have done his own dirty work,' sniffed the camel.

'As if I could be bribed by gifts of honey,' said the lion loftily.

The polar bear, even more lonely now, stayed on the roof of the ark and refused to come down. Mr Noah, quite upset, had a long talk to God.

'I don't know what to do about it,' he said. 'The polar bear can't stay up there for the whole of the voyage. Besides, I don't like the thought of him being unhappy.'

God thought for a moment. 'Go to the polar bear,' he said, 'and tell him that he won't make friends until he stops being so self-centred. If he wants friends, he must think of others rather than himself.'

'Well,' said Mr Noah doubtfully. 'I'll tell him, of course, but I don't think it will do any good.'

'Tell him that friendship cannot be bought,' said God. 'If it's not freely given then it's not real friendship.'

'All right,' said Mr Noah, getting up from his bed.

'And Noah,' said God, 'this is most important. Tell him that I am his friend—as I am the friend of *all* living creatures.'

Mr Noah climbed up to the roof of the ark and told the polar bear what God had said. He had to shout to make himself heard above the noise of the wind and rain. But the polar bear hardly listened. He just hunched his shoulders and turned away.

Sadly, Mr Noah began to leave. The rain was lashing down and the roof of the ark was very slippery. He took a step, then slipped on the wet surface. He slithered right down the steep slope and fell off, straight into the deep waters below.

'Help!' he shouted as he fell. 'Help, I can't swim! Please, someone—HELP!!'

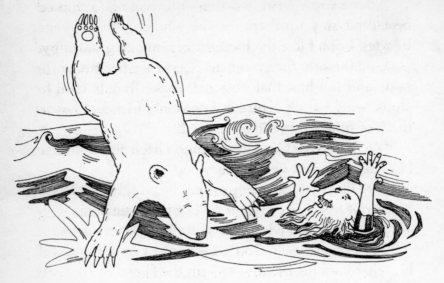

The polar bear heard him. He turned, jumped up, dived into the water and caught Mr Noah in his strong teeth before he sank beneath the waves. The animals, hearing the commotion, streamed out of the great hall and crowded up to the roof.

They saw the polar bear swimming with powerful strokes back to the ark. The giraffe bent his long neck and took the dripping wet Mr Noah from the polar bear. Then the kangaroo kept him warm in her pouch while she took him down to his cabin, where Mrs Noah put him to bed.

Later that evening the lion and the tiger went on to the roof.

'Er ... hmm ...' said the lion. The polar bear turned around.

'We've come,' said the lion, 'on behalf of the other animals. They sent us to tell you that we are all sorry for treating you in the way we did. If you would care to come down to the great hall, we would be honoured to be your friends.'

The polar bear swallowed hard.

'Really?' he asked.

'Really,' the tiger assured him.

'All of you?' asked the polar bear, not quite believing him.

'All of us,' said the lion solemnly.

'You were very brave,' the tiger added.

'I wasn't brave at all,' said the polar bear humbly. 'I can't help being a good swimmer. But Mr Noah was the only one who seemed to care about me and I couldn't let him drown.'

Warmly tucked up in his bed, and none the worse for his ordeal, Mr Noah was talking to God.

'Did you make me fall off the roof of the ark deliberately, God, so that the polar bear would rescue me?'

'Would I do a thing like that?' said God reproachfully.

Mr Noah smiled, turned over and went to sleep.

4

THE BUTTERFLY'S TALE

The rain fell, day after day, and the world was flooded. Earth and sky disappeared in a thick grey fog and it grew very cold. The wind howled, there were rumblings of thunder and flashes of lightning, but the ark, which God had told Mr Noah to build, remained afloat. Mr Noah, Mrs Noah, their sons and wives and two of every animal, insect and bird were safe and dry inside.

The sky grew black and it was dark inside the ark. Mr Noah lit lamps, but did not light many for fear of running out of oil.

The butterflies were unhappy in the dark and their brilliantly coloured wings grew dull and lifeless.

'How long do you think it will go on for?' asked one butterfly.

'Mr Noah said that it would rain for forty days and forty nights,' her husband replied.

'And how long has it already been raining?'

'I don't know,' said her husband. 'I never thought to count.'

'What's the point in counting?' said the grasshopper gloomily. 'It won't make the time pass any faster.'

'That's true.' The butterfly turned to his wife. 'Try to sleep,' he said. He touched his wife's delicate blue wings. 'You're shivering.'

'I'm cold,' she said.

'Tuck yourself under my wings,' her husband said, 'and I'll keep you warm.'

Soon he was fast asleep, but his wife remained awake. She looked up at the window in the great hall and watched with fearful eyes as the storm clouds grew thicker and the rain thudded against the roof.

'It's like night out there,' she whispered, but her husband slept on and did not hear her.

'I'm scared of the dark,' she whispered, but her husband only sighed and fluttered his wings in his sleep.

Mr Noah, making his round of the animals, insects and birds, heard the butterfly and hurried to her side.

'There's nothing to be afraid of,' he said gently. 'We're here because God wants us to be saved from the flood. He'll protect us and keep us from harm.'

'Yes,' said the butterfly. 'I know. But I'm still scared of the dark. I need the light in order to live. My cousin, the moth, flies at night, but butterflies fly in the sunshine.'

Mr Noah thought for a moment. 'I know,' he said. 'I'll

bring you an oil lamp and you can look at its flame and think of the sun. Would you like that?'

'Yes, please,' said the butterfly.

So Mr Noah went to his cabin and picked up his own lamp.

'Do you think this will help, God?' he asked anxiously.

'It might,' said God. 'And it's a kind thought.'

'Well, I can do without it,' said Mr Noah stoutly. But he looked round a little fearfully as the dark shadows seemed to leap from the walls of his cabin when he carried the oil lamp away.

The butterfly was grateful.

'Thank you,' she said. 'It's warm as well as light.'

'Yes it is,' said Mr Noah. 'But be careful now that you don't go too close or else you'll burn your wings.'

'I won't,' said the butterfly, and for a time she was happy as she stared deep into the flame. She pretended that it was a summer's day and that she was in a bright garden, basking in the warmth of the sun. But all too soon the oil ran out, the flame flickered and died and the butterfly was frightened once more.

'Mr Noah,' she called. 'Mr Noah. Could I have some more oil, please?'

But Mr Noah shook his head. 'I'm very sorry,' he said, 'but there really isn't any to spare. God told me exactly how much to bring and we've got just enough.'

'Oh dear,' the butterfly said fearfully.

'I'll talk to God and see if he can think of anything,' promised Mr Noah.

So Mr Noah went to his cabin and sat in the darkness and talked to God. The rain thudded on the roof and the wind whistled mournfully. Mr Noah shivered.

'I'm not surprised the butterfly is frightened, God,' he said. 'I'm a bit scared myself. Ever since I got locked in the woodshed by mistake and had to stay there all night, I've not really liked the dark.'

'If you're frightened, Noah,' said God, 'just remember that I created night as well as day. I am God of the dark as well as the light. I will never leave you to face the fears of the night alone.'

'Yes, God,' said Mr Noah, feeling a bit happier. 'I'll remember that. I'll tell the butterfly that, too.'

He went to tell the butterfly straight away, but she just looked at him with her big scared eyes. Mr Noah did not know what to do.

'Why don't you ask one of the other animals to help?' said God.

'Like who?' asked Mr Noah.

'One who isn't afraid of the dark,' said God.

'I don't know of any,' said Mr Noah.

'Think, Noah,' God said.

So Mr Noah sat in his cabin and thought.

'I know,' he said. 'There are her cousins, the moths.

They might help.'

He found the moths flying round and round the flame of one of the oil lamps, darting in and away, each time flying closer.

'You want to be careful,' Mr Noah said. 'You could get burnt.'

'Pooh,' said one of the moths. 'We're not frightened.'

'It's a good game,' said the other moth.

'It's very dangerous,' said Mr Noah.

'Well, everyone needs a bit of danger in their lives,' said the first moth.

'There's danger you can avoid, and danger you can't,' said Mr Noah sternly. He picked up the lamp and blew it out. 'I'm sorry, but I'm responsible for you while you're on the ark and God wants both of you safe at the end of the voyage.'

'Spoilsport,' said the second moth.

'I came to see if you would help me,' said Mr Noah. 'The butterfly is very unhappy. She's afraid of the dark. I thought that perhaps you might talk to her and reassure her that the dark needn't be frightening.'

'Why should we help you when you wouldn't let us play our game?' asked the first moth crossly.

'Because she's your cousin,' said Mr Noah. 'And because we've all got to help each other during this voyage if we're to survive.'

'Oh, go away and ask someone else,' said the second moth disagreeably.

So Mr Noah went away and talked to God once more.

'That idea didn't work, did it?' he said.

'There are other night animals besides moths, Noah,' said God.

'I suppose so,' said Mr Noah wearily. 'But it's a bit difficult finding them in the dark.'

Just then Mr Noah felt, rather than heard, a faint rustling of wings and he saw a dark shape hanging upside down at the end of his bed.

'Did someone want me?' came a soft voice.

'Of course!' said Mr Noah. 'Yes please, bat. I think you

41

might be just what's needed!'

'Now,' said the bat to the butterfly. 'What's this Mr Noah tells me?'

'I'm afraid of the dark,' said the butterfly in a small voice.

'But the dark is beautiful,' said the bat. 'As I fly though the night, it's like flying through velvet.'

'How do you see where you're going?' asked the butterfly.

'I don't need to see,' said the bat. 'I hear instead. Come with me. I'll take you to the darkest places on the ark and you'll see that there's nothing to be frightened about.'

The butterfly climbed hesitantly onto the back of the bat.

'Where are you going?' asked the owl. He blinked at her solemnly.

'The bat's showing me that there's nothing to fear from the dark,' said the butterfly.

'Nothing to fear? Of course there's nothing to fear,' came the brisk voice of the badger, speaking from a corner of the great hall. 'The dark, when the world is quiet and still, is the best time of all. It's the time for thinking.'

'I didn't know you could think,' snuffled the aardvark. 'I find the night-time best because the ants and termites are asleep so I can creep up on them unawares. And very tasty they are too,' he said licking his lips.

'Well, I like the night-time because it's safer,' croaked

the frog.

'So do I,' agreed the hedgehog.

'And my skin doesn't dry out as it would do in the sun,' the frog continued.

'I like it because it's cooler,' said the gerbil. 'In the desert, I always burrow into the ground during the day.'

'So you see, lots of us prefer the night,' the badger told the butterfly.

The hedgehog came close to the butterfly. 'It's really very nice of you to come and see us,' she said shyly. 'We don't often see such beautiful creatures at night.'

The bat took the butterfly to all the darkest corners on the ark and, as she met more of the animals, insects and birds that are awake at night, she saw that there was nothing at all to fear. At last she met the two moths.

'Hello,' she said shyly. 'I don't think we've met before.'

'Hmm,' said the first moth. 'So you're the one that got us into trouble with Mr Noah.'

'Trouble?'

'Yes,' said the other moth. 'He blew out the oil lamp

we were playing with.'

'Oh, I am sorry,' said the butterfly.

'Don't be sorry for them,' said the bat. 'They're just stupid. If it wasn't for Mr Noah, they'd have been burnt by the flame.'

He flew off, leaving the moths staring after him in surprise.

The butterfly slipped back into her place beside her husband. 'Thank you for taking me,' she said to the bat. 'I feel a lot better now.'

'It's been a great pleasure,' said the bat and flew away. The butterfly folded her wings and prepared to go to sleep. But just then she saw the glow of two faint lights.

'Mr Noah said you were frightened, so we thought we'd come and give you some light,' said one of the glow-worms.

'How kind of you,' said the butterfly. 'How kind everyone has been.'

The glow-worms stationed themselves one on either side of her, and the butterfly watched their comforting light and thought about the friends she had made in the darkness until she fell fast asleep.

Outside, the darkness began to lift and the light of day flooded in, although the rain continued without ceasing.

5

THE PARROT'S TALE

When God decided that he would send a flood to destroy the world, he told Mr Noah that it would rain for forty days and forty nights. The first of the great storms turned the sky black and it became as dark as night inside the small ark which housed Mr Noah, Mrs Noah, their sons, their wives and two of every animal, insect and bird. Many slept during the darkest days, but woke up when the sky grew lighter and the storm lifted.

'Is it over?' hissed the snake, slithering out of a hole.

'Is what over?' the elephant asked.

'The rain, of course.'

'Of course it's not over,' said the fox. 'Can't you hear it pounding on the roof?'

The snake listened for a moment. 'I can't hear anything.'

'That's because you're deaf,' said the fox.

'I'm not deaf,' said the snake, coiling himself neatly into a pyramid.

The fox grinned, then whispered, 'You are.'

'What was that you said?' the snake asked suspiciously.

The animals burst out laughing.

'Quiet everyone!' came the voice of Mr Noah, speaking from the shadows at the far end of the great hall. The laughter stopped.

'If you don't behave, there won't be double rations of food.'

'Are there to be double rations of food?' asked one of the pigs anxiously. The pigs were always anxious about food.

'Only if you behave.'

For the rest of the day the snake and the fox and all the animals, insects and birds on the ark behaved very well indeed. Only the monkey, scratching himself for the fleas who had decided to make a temporary home in his fur, was scornful.

'Bribing you, that's what Mr Noah's doing,' he said sourly. He scratched a bit harder. 'And if you fleas don't hop it quick, there'll be some very bad behaviour from me, double rations or no double rations!'

'Misery-guts!' said one of the fleas and they jumped onto the hedgehog's back.

At feeding time, Mr Noah and his three sons Shem, Ham and Japheth, came round with the food.

'What's this?' asked the pig, rooting around in his sty.

'This isn't double rations.'

'Neither's this,' said the fox. 'Come on, Mr Noah. What about your promise?'

'What promise?'

'You promised double rations if we behaved.'

'When did I promise that?' Mr Noah asked.

'This morning,' said the fox.

'Everyone heard you,' added the pig.

'Well, I'm very sorry,' said Mr Noah. 'But you must have dreamed it, for I never said anything of the sort.' He turned to his sons. 'Did you?'

His sons shook their heads.

'Well!' said the emu, after Mr Noah and his sons had gone. 'Words fail me!'

'Me too,' said the pig gloomily.

'I needn't have wasted all day trying to be good,' hissed the snake sadly.

'I never thought Mr Noah would stoop to such low-down tricks,' said the fox.

The jackal shook his head. 'It's just what I've always said. Never trust a human.'

'Stop tickling!' said the hedgehog. But he was speaking to the fleas so no one took any notice.

There was much grumbling that evening as the animals, insects and birds ate their meal and settled down for the night. But high up in the rafters of the great hall the parrot was laughing. He laughed so much that he nearly fell off his perch.

'That's confused them,' he said to his wife. 'Did you ever hear such a fuss?'

'It's very naughty of you,' his wife replied. 'You really shouldn't do it.'

'It's only a bit of fun.'

'It's not fun at all. It's making mischief.'

'Oh, don't be so miserable,' the parrot said crossly. He cleared his throat, then spoke in Mr Noah's voice.

'Lion,' he said. 'Tiger. Would you both come to my cabin. I've some very important things to discuss with you.' He cackled with laughter and said in his own voice. 'That'll upset them all right. Silly old things.'

A very surprised Mr Noah opened the door of his cabin to the lion and the tiger.

'Hello,' he said. 'What can I do for you?'

'What can *we* do for *you*?' the lion asked.

'What do you mean?' said Mr Noah.

'You asked us to come,' said the tiger. 'So we came.'

'No, I didn't,' said Mr Noah, confused.

The lion and tiger looked at one another.

'You said you had important things to discuss with us,' said the lion.

'Well, I'm sorry,' said Mr Noah, a bit crossly. 'But I haven't anything, important or otherwise, to discuss with you.'

And he closed the door of his cabin.

'I knew it,' said the lion as he and the tiger trotted away. 'It had to come. The strain of it is beginning to tell. Mr Noah is going mad. I said all along that he wasn't strong enough. God really should have put me in charge.'

'Or me,' said the tiger.

The parrot continued to mimic Mr Noah's voice. He also mimicked some of the other animals' voices. Soon everyone grew very cross and there were all sorts of arguments and fights. The parrot watched from his perch high above the great hall and enjoyed the trouble he was causing.

'Just look at them,' he said, hooting with delight and flapping his wings up and down. 'Look at the fuss they're in. Mr Noah too. I'm cleverer than all of them.'

'You must stop this,' said his wife. 'It's very childish.'

'Don't be so silly,' the parrot retorted.

'It's also unkind,' said his wife.

'It's not unkind. It's a good laugh.'

'Only for you,' said his wife. But the parrot took no notice.

Mr Noah became most alarmed at what was happening and had a serious talk to God. 'What's going on, God?' he asked. 'And what can I do about it? I must do something or there'll be a riot on board. I thought at first it was the lion, but now I'm not so sure.'

The door to his cabin opened and the parrot's wife flew in.

'I'm so sorry to disturb you, Mr Noah,' she said. 'But I've tried talking to him and it does no good. I'm really ashamed of all the trouble he's causing...'

After she had finished her story, Mr Noah went to the parrot and gave him a good telling-off. He was very cross, and so were the animals, insects and birds when they heard about it.

The parrot sulked on his perch.

'It was only meant as a bit of fun,' he said. 'I don't know why everyone's taken it so badly.'

'It wasn't a bit of fun and you know it,' his wife said severely.

The parrot glowered at her. 'If you hadn't gone and told Mr Noah, he'd never have known,' he said crossly.

'He would,' said his wife. 'When I went in, he was discussing it with God.'

'Why does God talk to Mr Noah and not to me?' the parrot asked.

'Because God's no fool and you *are*,' his wife said shortly.

The parrot was not listening. 'What makes Mr Noah so important that he can have a conversation with God?' he thought to himself. 'It can't be because he's clever for I'm sure I'm as clever as him. And it's not his voice,

because he's got rather a boring voice.' He sat on his perch and watched Mr Noah. 'I know,' he said out loud. 'It's because he wears clothes. *That's* why God talks to him. He wears clothes and we don't. Hmm...' and he grew very thoughtful.

'Just what are you plotting now?' his wife asked suspiciously, but the parrot flew away without replying.

It was some time before she saw him again. And when she did, she barely recognized him. For the parrot, waddling self-consciously into the great hall, was dressed. He was wearing a strange assortment of clothes taken from Mr and Mrs Noah's cabins. On his head was a long red and white scarf, tied like a turban, and round his body hung a shapeless brown gown. His clawed feet were thrust into sandals.

The parrot looked at his wife. 'Now I'll be able to talk to God,' he said with some satisfaction. But when he tried to fly up to his perch, the sandals fell off his feet with a thud and the animals, insects and birds in the great hall turned to stare. They stared, then they smiled, then they laughed. They laughed so much that they had to hold on to one another and some of them rolled around the great hall, shaking with mirth.

'What's so funny?' asked the parrot, but no one had the breath to tell him.

The noise brought Mr Noah running to the great hall. When he saw the parrot he had to smile, but tried not to laugh.

'So that's where my robe has gone,' he said mildly.

'I didn't mean to steal it,' the parrot said, hurriedly throwing off the borrowed clothes. 'I thought that if I wore clothes then I could talk to God like you and he would talk to me.'

Mr Noah looked round the grinning animals. 'Come with me,' he said to the parrot.

They went to his cabin and sat on the bed. 'I don't know why God speaks to me,' Mr Noah said once they were alone. 'But it's not because I wear clothes.'

'Oh,' said the parrot, surprised.

Mr Noah held out his hand and, after a moment, the parrot flew up and perched on it.

'It's not because I'm clever either,' Mr Noah went on. 'I'm nowhere near as clever as you with your different voices.'

'I see,' said the parrot.

'God made us all different and gave us all different gifts,' Mr Noah said. 'My family can talk to God, but we have to wear clothes as we don't have beautiful feathers like you to keep us warm. We can't fly either, although I've often wished I could.'

'Have you?' asked the parrot.

Mr Noah stroked the parrot's bright feathers and, after a moment or two, the parrot flew up to Mr Noah's shoulder.

'I'm sorry,' the parrot said. 'I've been an awful nuisance and caused a lot of trouble.'

'I don't mind you mimicking me,' Mr Noah said. 'So long as you let everyone know in advance.' He thought for a moment. 'Why don't you give us an evening's entertainment?'

The parrot brightened at the thought.

'Could I?' he asked.

'Yes,' said Mr Noah. 'You go and talk it over with your wife.'

'I haven't been very nice to her, either,' the parrot said uncomfortably.

'I know,' said Mr Noah. 'God told me.'

As the parrot was about to fly away, Mr Noah had another thought. 'If you would like to be here when I talk to God, you're very welcome to come and sit on my shoulder,' he said.

'Thank you,' the parrot said. 'I'd really like that.'

That evening the parrot and his wife entertained the animals, insects and birds in the great hall. It was a huge success and their lion and tiger impersonations caused many of the animals to cry with laughter, although the lion was not greatly amused.

The applause at the end of the show drowned out the sound of the wind and rain and echoed over the empty seas as the little ark floated on.

6

THE WOODWORM'S TALE

The cow opened her mouth and yawned, a big, wide, yawn. 'Oh dear ... I'm so ... ooo ... tired!'

'It's all this lazing about, doing nothing,' said the jackal dryly.

'I never do much anyway,' the cow replied comfortably. 'But it's not that. It's the noise. It's been keeping me awake at night.' She yawned again. 'Sorry, dears.'

'What noise?' asked the snake.

'I don't know,' the cow replied.

'Must be the rain,' said the jackal.

'It's not the rain. I'm used to the rain.'

'Well, it must have been the pigs then. They make dreadful grunting noises when they sleep.'

'It's not that either,' the cow said.

'What does it sound like?' asked the dormouse.

The cow considered. 'Like ... tapping. In the wall.'

The lion, who liked to order others around, walked

to the centre of the great hall.

'QUIET EVERYONE!' he roared.

The animals, insects and birds on board the ark all turned to look at him. The tiger opened one sleepy eye.

'What's he on about now?' he asked.

'The cow has heard a tapping noise in the walls of the ark,' said the lion. 'I want you all to be *absolutely* quiet and listen hard.'

The chatter, the grunts, the snuffles and the squeakings stopped as everyone listened hard.

'A ... A ... TISHOO ... !' The dingo sneezed loudly, then looked round apologetically. 'I'b awfully sorry everyone, bud I can't help id. I thig I'b god a cold.'

'Well, go away and sneeze somewhere else,' said the lion crossly.

'Not near me!' cried the emu in alarm. 'I don't want your nasty germs!'

The lion again called for quiet, but it was no use. The great hall was once more full of noise.

'We'll just have to listen tonight,' the lion said to the cow.

That night the lion, the tiger, the jackal, the dog and many other interested animals crowded into the cow's byre and put their ears to the wall.

'There it is!' breathed the flamingo excitedly. 'Tap, tap, tap.'

'Do you think someone's trying to get in?' asked the donkey anxiously.

'Of course not,' scoffed the jackal. 'There's only fish outside the ark and they wouldn't want to get in.'

'Wouldn't they?' said the donkey, rather surprised.

'Perhaps someone's trying to get out.' suggested the llama.

'Possibly,' said the lion after giving it much thought.

Just then a reddish-brown head popped out from inside the wall.

' 'ello,' it said. 'Can you help me? I have lost my friend. We went tunnelling together but 'e went zat way and I went zis and now I can't find 'im.'

'Who are you?' asked the lion.

'I am ze furniture beetle,' said the creature. 'Ow do you do?' The head disappeared for a moment then re-emerged. 'Sorry,' it said. 'I have to go. I think I see ze tunnel of my friend.'

And with that it disappeared for good.

The following morning, Rachel, Shem's wife, arrived in the cow's byre, carrying the milking stool and pail.

'Good morning,' she said. 'It's a lovely morning, or it would be, if it stopped raining. How are you this morning?'

'Terrible dear,' said the cow placidly. 'Didn't get a wink of sleep last night. Tap, tap, tap all night long.'

57

'Oh, I'm sorry,' said Rachel. She put down the stool. 'What was tapping?'

'Some beetle or other,' said the cow. 'I didn't take much notice. Most of the animals on the ark were in here and I had an awful job getting rid of them.'

'Dear, dear.' Rachel positioned the pail, sat down on the stool ... and fell on the floor with a bump! The stool had collapsed underneath her and was now in pieces on the floor.

'Well, I never!'

'Are you all right?' asked the cow, concerned.

'I think so,' said Rachel, gingerly getting to her feet and rubbing her sore behind. She picked up the pieces of the stool and looked at them closely. 'This stool is riddled with holes! Whatever can have caused them?'

A reddish-brown head appeared out of one of the holes.

'I did,' it said brightly. ' 'Ave you seen my friend?'

High up in the great hall, the parrot was swinging on his perch practising his many different voices when there was a cracking noise. The parrot gave a shriek as the perch broke, and he flew across the hall in alarm.

'Shiver me timbers and splice me mainbrace, what hit me?'

' 'Allo,' said a reddish-brown head poking its way out of the fallen piece of wood. 'I have lost my friend. 'Ave you seen her?'

Then he turned and disappeared.

'The time has come,' said the lion, 'when we have to act!'

'Absolutely, old chap,' said the parrot, imitating the lion's voice.

'Otherwise the ark won't be safe for anyone,' the lion continued, ignoring the interruption. 'Those beetles, or whatever they call themselves, have got to be stopped!'

'Woodworm,' said the jackal.

'What?' asked the lion.

'That's what they are. Woodworm. They eat through wood.'

There was a sudden silence in the great hall as the animals, insects and birds looked at each other. The wooden structure of the ark, which had seemed so safe when they were first on board, now appeared very fragile. They could hear the rain pounding on the roof and the wind howling outside. The ark dipped and swayed in the choppy seas.

'Holes!' the emu shrieked. 'I can see thousands of holes! The ark's going to collapse!'

'I knew something like this would happen,' said the monkey in an I-told-you-so voice. 'This whole trip was doomed from the start.'

'I think we should tell Mr Noah what's happened,' said the badger in a practical voice.

'Just what I was going to suggest,' the lion said quickly. 'Tiger, shall we go?'

When the lion and tiger reached Mr Noah's cabin, they found that he already knew told about the woodworm. Rachel had shown him her broken stool. He hurried to the great hall, the lion and tiger on either side.

'What are you going to do, Mr Noah?' the jackal called to him.

'I don't know yet,' Mr Noah said, somewhat flustered. 'I shall have to think.'

'Well I wouldn't think for too long,' the monkey said sourly. 'Or the ark might fall to pieces.'

'Fleas are one thing,' said the hedgehog, busily scratching himself. 'I can put up with fleas. Woodworm's another.'

'First we must find the woodworms,' Mr Noah said. 'And for that we need absolute quiet ...'

In the silence that followed, everyone listened hard for the sound of tapping. But no one, not even the animals with the most sensitive hearing, could hear a thing.

'Perhaps they've gone to sleep,' suggested the badger.

'Or tunnelled their way outside and fallen into the water,' said the donkey, but no one really believed that. It was with some anxiety that everyone settled down for the night.

It was late when Mr Noah returned to his cabin and he was very tired. He threw himself on his bed and was soon fast asleep. But his sleep was disturbed by a dream that the ark was sinking. It sank lower and lower—and Mr Noah woke up in alarm.

'Help!' he called. 'What's happening?'

Then he realized. The foot of his bed had collapsed on to the floor.

'Tap ... tap ... tap ...'

'Is that you, woodworm?' Mr Noah asked crossly.

A reddish-brown head popped out of a hole in one of the wooden posts of Mr Noah's bed.

'Did someone call?'

'Have you just made my bed collapse?'

'But no!' said the woodworm. 'All I was doing was tunnelling to try and find my friend.' He shook his head sadly. 'But she is not 'ere. I go elsewhere to look.'

'Wait a minute,' said Mr Noah. 'How did you lose her?'

'We arrive on ze ark together,' said the woodworm. 'And we start tunnelling together also. We like to tunnel together. But we go tunnelling in ze wrong directions and we lose each other. It is very sad.'

'I think,' said Mr Noah, 'that the first thing to do is to find your friend. God will know where she is. We'll ask him for help.'

So he sat on the edge of his bed and asked God for help in finding the other woodworm.

There was a knock on his door. It was the dingo.

'Sorry to distub you, Bister Noah,' he said, his head full of cold. 'Bud I had by head out through the trab-door, trying to clear by doze, when I heard this tabbing...'

'Wait there,' Mr Noah said to the woodworm and he hurried to the roof of the ark.

'Tap ... tap ... tap tap ...'

'Is that you, woodworm?' Mr Noah asked.

'It is I,' said the woodworm, poking her head out.

'Come with me,' said Mr Noah. 'I've found your friend.'

Back in his cabin, Mr Noah watched the delighted reunion of the woodworms. But he was still worried.

'What do I do with them, God?' he asked. 'If I just let them go off making more holes, what will become of the ark?'

'You don't appear to have much faith in my plans, Noah,' God said reproachfully.

'Oh I do, God,' Mr Noah protested.

'Do you think I haven't given thought to the wood-worms? They are as much my creatures as you.'

Mr Noah sat silent.

'Why not ask *them*?' God suggested.

Mr Noah turned to the woodworms. 'Now that you've found each other, would you stop tunnelling, please?' he asked.

They looked at him in surprise. 'Stop tunnelling?' one of them said. 'Oh no, that is impossible.'

'But I'm worried about the safety of the ark,' Mr Noah said.

'Did you 'ere that? 'He's worried about ze safety of ze ark!'

'That is a good joke,' said the other one.

'Well, I don't think it's very funny,' Mr Noah said.

'Oh, but it is. The wood of the ark , Mr Noah, is so hard you would need an army of us all working together for a long, long time before there was any danger to ze ark.'

'That is why we chose softer wood, like ze stool and ze parrot's perch,' the other explained.

'And your bed,' added the first.

'I see,' said Mr Noah feeling much better. He picked up Rachel's broken stool. 'Would you agree to spend the rest of the voyage tunnelling through this stool? The other animals would be pleased, and it's nice soft wood. It would also mean that you wouldn't lose each other again.'

'That is a good idea,' said the first woodworm, nodding his reddish-brown head. 'We will do whatever you say.'

'Except stop tunnelling,' said the second woodworm.

'Except that, of course,' agreed the first.

Mr Noah went off to tell the animals in the great hall the good news. As he went, he could hear the distant tap, tap, tapping of the woodworms and, even more distantly, their conversation.

'No, it is this way we go . . .'

'No, this is better. Follow me . . .'

The sound of their talking and tapping died away until all Mr Noah could hear was the sound of the rain beating on the ark and the noise of the howling wind.

7
MRS NOAH'S TALE

Mrs Noah was not at all happy when her husband told her that God would send a flood to destroy the world, not even when he told her that she and their children and two of every creature in the world would be saved.

'It's not that I'm not grateful to God for saving us,' she said. 'Mind you, I'm not in the least surprised. You're a good man and I'm only glad to see that God recognizes the fact. He doesn't always seem to reward the good,' she added, with a disapproving sniff.

'Now, Becky, you mustn't talk like that about God,' Mr Noah said.

'I don't see why not,' said Mrs Noah. 'Anyway, that's not the point. The thing is, I don't want to go off in a boat, however well built it is—although knowing your carpentry, Noah, I doubt whether it'll stand up to much. I don't like boats and I think it's a bit unreasonable of God to plan all this without talking to us about it first.'

'He talked to me,' Mr Noah said.

'That's as may be,' Mrs Noah replied. 'But why didn't God speak to *me* as well? I could have given him some good advice.'

All Mr Noah could do was shrug his shoulders.

Mrs Noah sighed. 'God knew you'd give in to anything he said. You're soft as butter.'

'Becky, do you think I like leaving our farm like this any better than you do?' Mr Noah protested. 'But we can't go against God's will. He only wants the best for us.'

'That's as may be,' Mrs Noah said, pursing her lips.

She did not speak of it again, but she thought about it a great deal.

'It's not fair,' she thought. 'God never speaks to me, although I'm always on at him about one thing or another.' She frowned. 'Anyway, I think God should have managed better. If I'd been God, I wouldn't have let things get in such a mess in the first place. Sending a flood to destroy the world indeed! Such a waste!'

Mrs Noah was not happy on board. It was not so much the animals, or the cramped conditions, or even the rain that bothered her. It was just that she was not a good sailor and to be a sailor's wife was not what she had intended when she had married Mr Noah. So she spent a lot of time in her cabin, and although she cooked and cleaned and did all the work expected of her, she grew more and more depressed. Mr Noah became very worried and tried talking to her.

'You never smile, Becky,' he said. 'And you always used to.'

'There's nothing to smile about!' she snapped.

Mr Noah sighed. 'I know this is a lot of work and not much fun, but we should be thankful that we're alive.'

'Hmm!' Mrs Noah retorted.

Mr Noah went away and talked it over with God.

'She says that she gets seasick, but I don't think that's the real problem. I think she just doesn't trust you the way I do and that's what's making her so unhappy. Can't you talk to her?'

'She wouldn't listen if I did,' God said.

'Of course she would,' Mr Noah said eagerly. 'She's always saying that she talks to you but you never reply.'

'She doesn't talk *to* me, Noah,' God said rather sadly. 'She talks *at* me. But don't worry about her. Just leave everything to me.'

A few days later Mrs Noah found Japheth sitting by himself in a corner of the ark. Mrs Noah was very fond of all her sons and their wives, but Japheth, her youngest, was her especial favourite and she was worried when she found him in tears.

'Whatever's the matter?' she asked.

'Oh, Mum, I can't tell you. I can't tell anyone.'

'Of course you can. Now what is it?'

'Well, it's the wild animals,' Japheth confessed. 'I'm

scared of them. No, not just scared. I'm terrified. I've tried getting over it, honestly, but it doesn't get any better, it just gets worse. And I can't tell Shem or Ham because they'd only laugh and say I was being stupid. And I *am* being stupid, I know.'

Mrs Noah put her arms round him.

'The thought of being cooped up here for months, maybe longer, is just driving me crazy,' he said between sobs. 'But whenever I see that lion, my legs go all shaky. And when the tiger yawns and shows all those sharp teeth, I think about what it would be like if he began to eat me and then I feel sick all over. Oh, Mum, what can I do?'

Mrs Noah was silent for a moment. 'Have you talked to your father?' she asked at last.

'Dad?' Japheth sat up. 'Oh, I couldn't possibly tell him. He'd feel I was letting him down. I'd be so ashamed. You won't tell him, will you? Promise?'

'Not if you don't want me to,' she promised. 'Now why don't you go up on the roof and get a bit of fresh air and in the meantime I'll try and think of something.'

When he had gone Mrs Noah thought hard, but she could not think of anything, so at last she spoke to God.

'Now listen, God,' she said severely. 'You got us into this mess and it's your duty to help Japheth.'

God listened, but did not speak.

Over the next few days Japheth continued to do his

work, but some of the animals began to sense that
something was wrong.

'Do you know,' said the gorilla, 'I popped up and said
"boo" to him and he nearly fainted away on the spot!'

'Why did you do that?' asked the jackal. 'Seems rather
a silly thing to do.'

'I just thought it would be a bit of fun,' said the gorilla.
'You know, help to pass the time.'

The tiger smiled lazily. 'It is rather fun to frighten him,
I must admit,' he said. 'When I snapped my teeth the
other day I thought he'd have a heart attack.'

'Little things please little minds,' said the jackal. The
tiger sprang to his feet.

'Who are you calling little?' he asked in a dangerous voice.

'Oh, do lie down and be quiet,' said the jackal. 'You don't frighten me.'

'Personally, I think it's unkind to frighten the boy,' said the rhinoceros. 'He's harmless, isn't he?'

'Yes, but he's spineless,' said the wolf, baring his sharp teeth. 'I'd be ashamed of him if he was a cub of mine. He needs toughening up.'

'You won't do it by frightening him,' said the rhinoceros firmly.

'What he needs is your thick skin,' grinned the fox.

While the animals were discussing Japheth, Japheth himself was growing more and more frightened every time he had to enter the great hall. Hannah, his wife, asked if he was ill and Japheth clutched at this excuse gratefully and took to his bed. Meanwhile, Mrs Noah was busy on his behalf. Every day she spoke to God, demanding that he *do* something.

'All I'm asking, God, is that you give my poor son a bit of courage. It's not that much to ask, is it? I mean, I know you're busy flooding the world and everything, but you could take the time to give Japheth a bit of help. It wouldn't take you long. It's been a week now since I first spoke to you about it and what have you done? Nothing. I must say it's enough to shake anyone's faith!'

Just then Mr Noah came into the cabin.

'Whatever are you doing?' he asked.

'I'm giving God a piece of my mind,' Mrs Noah said firmly.

'Oh? Why?'

'Well,' Mrs Noah began, then remembered her promise to Japheth. 'Something has happened which God knows about and although I keep telling God to sort it out, I just don't think he wants to know.'

'Now Becky, you can't go *telling* God what to do. He knows better than we do what our needs are and he'll answer our prayers but in his own way and his own time.'

'That's all very well,' sniffed Mrs Noah. 'But there isn't much time and it seems to me that his way of answering is to do nothing.'

'I wouldn't be too sure about that,' Mr Noah said. 'What is the problem anyway?'

'I can't tell you. It was told to me in confidence.'

'It must be one of the boys in trouble,' Mr Noah said wisely. 'Look, why don't you try talking it over with God, instead of giving him orders? I don't like being ordered about and I don't suppose God does either.'

When he left, Mrs Noah sat alone in the cabin. At first she was cross with her husband, as cross as she was with God, but then she began to think about what he had said.

'Is he right, God?' she asked at last. 'Do I order you about?'

71

'Well, yes, you do,' God said.

'Is that *really* you, God?' Mrs Noah asked, surprised at being answered.

'Yes,' said God.

'Do I just give you lists of things I want done and expect you to do them?' Mrs Noah asked.

'I'm afraid so,' said God.

Mrs Noah thought about it some more.

'I'm sorry if I've been rude,' she said at last. 'It's just that I'm so worried. Nothing seems to have gone right, and you never talk to me like you talk to Noah.'

'I'm talking to you now,' said God.

'Yes,' said Mrs Noah. 'Thank you.'

She was silent for a moment, then said in a small voice. 'Please, would you help Japheth?'

'Of course,' said God. 'We'll help him together.'

Some time later, Mrs Noah went to the great hall. She walked straight through the teeming mass of animals to the lion and the tiger.

'Lion. Tiger. I need your help,' she said firmly.

'Delighted to oblige, dear lady,' said the lion graciously.

'Me too,' said the tiger, lazily scratching himself.

That evening, when most of the animals were asleep, Mrs Noah took a white and trembling Japheth by the hand into the great hall. The lion and the tiger were waiting for them.

'Now then,' she said to her son. 'There's really nothing at all to be afraid of. Look at them. They're just like big, soft cats.'

The lion winced, but the tiger only grinned and began to purr in a deep voice.

'I'm sorry I'm so stupid,' said Japheth, swallowing hard. 'But it's your teeth ... and your claws ... they make me afraid. You're both so strong.'

'Well I am the King of the Jungle,' said the lion, not displeased. 'Lord of all the Beasts. There's no harm, young man, in being afraid. It's quite sensible of you, really.'

'Really?' asked Japheth.

'Yes. Although we wouldn't hurt you.'

'Not a hair of your head,' added the tiger.

'You see, we made an agreement with Mr Noah that while we were on this voyage we wouldn't hunt other animals.'

'And certainly not eat them,' put in the tiger, a righteous expression on his face.

'So you're absolutely safe,' said the lion.

The tiger held out his paw. 'Shake on it,' he said.

Japheth looked at the sharp claws and gulped. Then he put out his hand and solemnly shook the tiger's paw, then the lion's.

'I feel better,' he said.

'You're a good lad,' said the lion. 'Don't you worry. We'll look after you.'

Japheth smiled and went to bed.

'Thank you, God,' Mrs Noah said when she was back in her cabin.

'Any time,' said God. 'Oh, and Becky . . .'

'Yes?'

'Are you still unhappy about being on the ark?'

'I haven't had time to think about it,' Mrs Noah said. And she smiled.

8

THE PANDA'S TALE

When the animals, insects and birds first boarded the ark, Mr Noah had taken great pains to make them all as comfortable as possible. God had told him what food to provide and whether the animals were more at home hanging upside down from the rafters—like the bats—hiding in crevices—like the geckos—or wallowing in mud — like the hippos. Mr Noah had tried to make living and sleeping areas on the ark to suit all the different tastes. But when it came to the two pandas, Mr Noah scratched his head and was stuck. God had not told him much about them, other than that they ate bamboo shoots and did not need anywhere special to sleep.

When the pandas arrived on board they took Mr Noah to one side.

'I don't like other animals,' said the male panda gruffly. 'Never know what to say to them.'

'I see,' said Mr Noah.

'I don't like them either,' said the female panda. 'They're very loud.'

'Not all of them,' said Mr Noah.

The female panda stared at him with her big dark eyes. 'I prefer to keep myself to myself,' she said.

'Isn't that a bit lonely?' asked Mr Noah.

'I don't know,' said the female panda. 'I've never really thought about it. I've always been on my own.'

'Could you tell me,' said the male panda loudly, 'where my range is to be?'

'Your range?' repeated Mr Noah.

'Yes. My territory—the part of the ark where I can roam about quite freely and quite alone?'

Mr Noah was mystified. 'But both of you can go anywhere,' he said. 'Together or separately.'

The pandas shook their heads.

76

'Not together,' said the female panda firmly. 'I roam on my own.'

'So do I,' said the male panda.

'Well, if that's what you want ...' Mr Noah began doubtfully.

'Oh, it is,' the male panda assured him. 'We prefer to be quite separate.'

'Very well,' said Mr Noah. 'But you'll come to the welcome meeting in the great hall tonight, won't you?'

The male panda shook his head. 'No,' he said. 'Not for me.'

'Me neither,' said the female panda, and they both turned away from Mr Noah and went off in different directions.

Mr Noah hardly ever saw them after that first day. Sometimes he or his sons caught glimpses of one or other as they made their way along a corridor or up some stairs. But usually the only signs he had that the pandas were still on the ark were the shredded remains of bamboo which he put out for their food. Whenever the other animals tried to talk to them, the pandas just walked off without saying a word.

'Don't they need friends?' marvelled the polar bear as he caught sight of a large black-and-white shape disappearing down the corridor.

'Obviously not,' said his wife comfortably.

'Well, well,' said the polar bear, shaking his head. 'I

don't know whether or not to feel sorry for them.'

Other animals were more outspoken.

'It's not natural,' sniffed the emu. 'If they don't want to mix with us that's fair enough, although I must say I do think it's rather stuck-up of them, but at least they should be together and not on their own. My husband and I are always together, aren't we, dear?'

Her husband nodded, but said, a little wistfully, 'It might be nice to be on one's own from time to time.'

'Nonsense,' said the emu briskly. 'You'd hate it. Anyway,' she continued, 'it shouldn't be allowed. Mr Noah should tell them that their behaviour might be all right in China or wherever they come from, but it's not at all the thing on the ark.'

'Oh, leave them alone,' said the jackal impatiently. 'Sometimes I think the pandas have the right idea. At least they don't have to listen to others drivelling on all the time.' The emu did not hear this for she had bustled off to speak to Mr Noah.

The animals soon found a new subject to talk about and the pandas were forgotten. Day after day they walked slowly round and round the ark, their great heads swaying from side to side. They rarely met anyone, not even one another.

But after a while, the female panda began to feel curious. Although she never entered the great hall, which was always filled with animals, insects and birds of all shapes and sizes, she sometimes stood just outside the doorway and peered in. She saw twos, threes, whole groups of animals, talking together, playing games together, eating together. She saw them squabbling and laughing and sometimes fighting. The panda was amazed.

'Whatever do they talk about?' she wondered.

Pandas do not have regular sleeping places. They sleep whenever they feel tired and wherever they happen to be at the time. Sometimes they sleep during the day and sometimes during the night.

One night the female panda crept into the great hall. She walked quietly among the sleeping animals and gazed down at them. It was all very strange, she thought. Perhaps they liked being together.

And bit by bit the panda began to be curious about the other panda on the ark. She started to follow him and they met, by accident it seemed, a couple of times. But when she tried to talk to him, he just turned and plodded away, not hurriedly, but in a very determined manner. At last, not knowing what else to do, the panda went to see Mr Noah.

'I'm very sorry to trouble you,' she said.

'It's no trouble,' said Mr Noah. 'That's what I'm here for.'

'You see, I know I said that I preferred being on my own,' said the panda. 'Well, that was true. I did like it. I didn't know anything else. But now I've seen how the animals talk together and eat together and it looks rather nice.' She stopped.

'Yes?' said Mr Noah encouragingly.

'I think,' said the female panda, 'that I'd like to meet some of the other animals. It's very lonely being on your own.'

Mr Noah introduced the female panda to some of the animals in the great hall. Although shy at first, the panda was a great success for all the animals were curious about her.

'Why are your eyes ringed with black?' asked the swallow, flying down to look at her more closely.

'I don't know,' said the panda.

'It's not because you've been in a fight, is it?' the aardvark questioned.

'No. I've never been in a fight.'

'Don't be so personal,' said the warthog disapprovingly. 'I'm sure you wouldn't be too pleased if someone came and asked about your big nose.'

'I wouldn't mind,' said the aardvark. 'It's better than being all-over ugly like you.'

The warthog grinned amiably. He didn't mind what he looked like.

But despite her new friends, the female panda did not forget about the other panda, still roaming by himself around the ark.

'I mean, we're both pandas, we must have something in common. Things we can talk about,' she explained to Mr Noah. She thought for a moment. 'Like the kind of bamboo shoots we like eating.'

'Perhaps he's shy,' said Mr Noah. 'Why don't you invite him to tea with Mrs Noah and myself?'

'I'll do that,' said the female panda. But when she went to look for the panda, she could not find him. More worrying, none of the bamboo left for him to eat had been touched for at least three days.

She hurried to find Mr Noah.

'Wherever can he be?' she asked in alarm.

'I don't know,' said Mr Noah. 'But if he's on the ark, we'll find him.'

He organized a search party and he and the animals looked everywhere.

But it was the female panda, knowing the kind of places the panda would prefer, who eventually found him, in pitch darkness, right down in the hold of the ark, at the bottom of a steep ladder.

'I slipped and hurt my leg,' he said to the female panda, 'and I couldn't climb back up again. I *am* hungry.'

The female panda tried to lift him but he was too heavy for her.

'I'll go and get help,' she promised.

She found Mr Noah and he and the animals rushed to the top of the ladder and peered down into the darkness.

'Are you badly hurt?' Mr Noah asked.

'No,' said the panda curtly. 'Just my leg. If you could give me a hand out I'd be grateful.'

The two gorillas, who were very strong, swung themselves down the ladder and formed a chain with the polar bear and the lion. Together they lifted the panda out of the hold.

After a good meal and some first aid on his leg, the panda got to his feet.

'Thanks for the rescue and everything,' he said gruffly to Mr Noah. 'Much appreciated. I must be off now.'

'Must you?' Mr Noah asked mildly.

'Oh yes.' The panda looked slowly around the great hall, which was noisy and crowded. 'I'm a loner.'

The female panda glanced at him.

'I thought I was too,' she said. 'But I've changed my mind. We all need each other. Look what happened to you. You would have died if we hadn't found you.'

'Maybe,' said the panda. 'But I'm better on my own.' He shrugged. 'I can't change my nature.'

'No,' said Mr Noah. 'But God can.' He smiled at them both and quietly walked away.

A few days later, as he was carrying the evening meal from the kitchen to the great hall, Mr Noah saw not one, but two pandas walking slowly away from him down the corridor, their great heads swaying contentedly together from side to side.

'Thank you, God,' Mr Noah said. 'I knew you would help.'

He was still smiling as he walked into the great hall.

'I don't know what there is to smile about,' said the monkey sourly. 'It's still raining, isn't it?'

'Oh yes,' said Mr Noah. 'It's still raining. But it's been a lovely day for all that.'

9

THE GIRAFFE'S TALE

It was the thirty-ninth day of the voyage. Thirty-nine days had passed since God sent the rain which had flooded the world, and on every one of those days Mr Noah or one of his sons had placed a large cross on a chart in the great hall of the ark. Each day the animals, insects and birds had crowded around—although few of them could read—to see how many days of rain were left.

'Now let me see,' said the owl, staring at the chart with unblinking eyes, 'it's been raining for thirty-nine days.'

'Is that all?' remarked the jackal gloomily. 'It seems like a lifetime.'

'And God said it would rain for forty days. That means . . .' The owl, who liked doing sums, did a hurried calculation. 'That means there's only one day of rain left,' he finished triumphantly.

'Depends whether you've counted the nights,' said the monkey.

'What do you mean?'

'Mr Noah told us that God said it would rain for forty days and forty nights,' explained the monkey. He grinned sarcastically. 'You've only counted the days.'

'Does that mean,' asked the giraffe, who was inclined to be a bit slow, 'that after tomorrow it will have rained for forty days, and then it's got to rain for forty nights before it stops?'

'Of course it doesn't,' said the gorilla, who had ambled over to see what all the fuss was about.

'Why not?' asked the giraffe.

'Because we've been asleep during the nights so we've missed it,' said the gorilla.

The giraffe shook his head. 'I don't understand,' he said, wrinkling his brow in a puzzled way.

'Never mind,' said the owl kindly. 'I wouldn't let it worry you.'

The animals, insects and birds were careful not to let things worry the giraffe as they knew that he was easily upset.

The giraffe did look anxious for a moment, then his face cleared. 'Did I ever tell you the story about the lake that wouldn't dry up?' he asked hopefully.

The animals sighed and settled down for what would be a long and not very funny story. But no one complained because everyone liked the giraffe. Only the dog remained, staring in a troubled way at the chart.

'Thirty-nine and one is...' she said to herself in a puzzled voice. 'Thirty-nine and one is...' The dog was very bad at sums.

When two of every animal, insect, reptile and bird had first entered the ark, Mr Noah had been amazed at the variety of God's creation. There were tall ones, short ones, thin ones and fat ones. Some were plain, some were ugly, some were handsome, and some, as Mr Noah afterwards said to his wife, were downright peculiar.

'But then,' he added, 'God made us all different. It would be boring if we were all alike.'

But of all the animals who entered the ark, Mr Noah found the giraffes the oddest.

'With those long necks and small heads, I wasn't sure the ark would be tall enough for them, but it is... just,' Mr Noah said. 'I'm glad I followed God's advice in building it, and didn't try to cut any corners.'

There were not many places on the ark where the giraffes could stand and stretch their necks with any comfort but, as the giraffe's wife said placidly, 'We're a lot better off than some of the heavier animals, poor things.' She glanced at the two elephants. 'At least we don't make the ark tilt from side to side when we walk.'

The giraffe's wife was not as tall as her husband. When she walked she picked her way carefully among the teeming animals on the ark. Her husband did not find it so easy.

'Hey, mind where you're going!' squeaked the dormouse in alarm as the giraffe almost squashed him.

'Oh, sorry,' said the giraffe.

'Watch out!' cried the guinea-pig.

'Oh dear,' said the giraffe. He put his front foot down on the ground . . . and lifted it hurriedly as it came into contact with the hedgehog. 'Owwh!' he yelled. He bent his long neck anxiously.

'Are you all right?' he asked the hedgehog.

'Oh yes, *I'm* all right,' said the hedgehog. 'But are *you* all right? I'm terribly sorry to have got in your way.'

'Some animals just don't look where they're going,' sniffed the emu.

'It's hardly his fault,' said the ant-eater. 'It must be difficult seeing where you're going when your head's in the air. I prefer to snuffle along the ground. Better for finding ants,' he added, licking his lips.

'Thanks for nothing,' said the ant.

'It *is* difficult,' the giraffe said earnestly. 'My wife manages all right, but then you see, I'm terribly clumsy. I always have been. It makes life very hard.'

He squinted at the ground before taking a cautious step forwards. It was a mistake. A loud squealing rose above the noise in the great hall.

'Say, I'd sure be grateful if you would—uh—remove yourself out of my sty,' said the pig. 'Honey here is trying to sleep.'

His wife grunted.

'I'm awfully sorry,' said the giraffe apologetically.

He moved to one side, which was another mistake.

There was a loud splash as he fell into the tank of water which was kept for the reptiles and animals who liked bathing.

The crocodiles snapped their jaws, missing the hippopotamus by inches. The hippo heaved himself hurriedly out of the way, which caused the ark to shudder under his great weight. The two elephants began to laugh, while the poor giraffe struggled to get out.

'Help! Get me out of here! Help!'

He slipped further into the tank and fell against the water buffalo, who was knocked sideways into the rhinoceros. A great tidal wave of water spurted up, soaking all the animals, insects and birds in the great hall. Everyone floundered around making a tremendous noise and Mr and Mrs Noah came running to see what had happened.

The giraffe was soon hauled out and stood upright again, dripping wet and very unhappy.

'I'm sorry,' he kept repeating. 'I'm so terribly sorry.'

He was so upset that no one could be angry for long.

'We should be grateful to you,' said the fox, shaking drops of water from his bushy tail, 'for brightening up a boring evening. There's not been much on-board entertainment provided on the ark.'

A large tear rolled off the end of the giraffe's nose and another followed it.

'There's no need to cry,' said the swallow, circling overhead. 'No one's blaming you.'

'I'm so stupid and so clumsy,' said the giraffe. 'I really don't know why God chose me to come on the ark. I should have been left behind to d-drown!'

Another tear rolled down his cheek.

'Oh, come on,' said the jackal. 'Cheer up. Worse things happen at sea.'

'We *are* at sea,' the lion reminded him.

Nothing anyone said was of any help to the giraffe. When he accidentally trod on the dog's tail, his mind was made up. He planted himself in the centre of the great hall and closed his eyes.

'You needn't worry any more,' he said. 'Any of you. I'll just stay here and not move until the journey is over. Just pretend I'm made of wood.'

And that was where Mr Noah found him, some hours later.

'Come along old thing,' Mr Noah said. 'You really can't stay there for the rest of the trip. You'll get cramp.'

'But if I move I might tread on someone,' said the giraffe. 'I'd rather have cramp than tread on someone.' His bottom lip trembled. 'I'm so clumsy, Mr Noah. And I'm such a ridiculous shape. It was all right when I was at home, but here I'm just useless and a menace to everyone.'

'No you're not,' said Mr Noah stoutly. 'Look, I'll go and talk to God. I'm sure he'll be able to help.'

'I know the ark's crowded, but he can't stand still for the rest of the voyage,' Mr Noah said, having told God the problem. 'I just don't know what the answer is.' He thought for a moment. 'What he needs is a job. Something to show him that he isn't useless.'

'That time will come,' God said. 'There will be a job for him later. Meanwhile, I suggest you speak to the animals. I'm sure they will help.'

So Mr Noah asked the animals for help. He spoke to the large animals, but it was the small ones who came up with the solution.

'If I fly beside the giraffe, I can warn him of danger,' said the swallow.

'And I can walk beside him, and call out if there's anyone in the way,' said the dormouse.

'I'll help,' offered the hedgehog.

'If the giraffe doesn't mind my sitting on his back, I can relay messages to him,' said the koala bear. 'I'm used to heights.'

The giraffe was overwhelmed by these offers of help.

'Thank you,' he said. 'Thank you all.'

The animals took up their positions.

'Make way, there, make way,' called the dog

importantly. 'The giraffe is about to move!'

'Left a bit,' said the dormouse as the giraffe took a hesitant step.

'Left a bit,' repeated the koala bear.

The giraffe moved to the left.

'Take care! There's a beetle right ahead,' called the swallow.

'Don't worry about me,' said the beetle. 'I can get out of the way. Just watch out for the centipede. He's over on your right.'

'Centipede on the right!' cried the hedgehog.

'Centipede on the right!' repeated the koala bear.

And the giraffe, with the help of his new friends, was able to move round the ark in safety.

On the fortieth day of the voyage the owl and many of the other animals watched Mr Noah make a large cross on the chart.

'Forty,' said the owl. 'It's the fortieth day.'

'Thirty-nine plus one is forty,' said the dog under her breath. 'Thirty-nine plus one is forty. I must remember that.'

The eagle suddenly swept down from the rafters.

'The rain,' he cried in a deep voice, 'has stopped!'

A great sigh went round the hall.

'God has kept his promise,' said Mr Noah.

He smiled at the hushed animals, insects and birds. When he saw the giraffe his smile suddenly grew broader.

'I've got it!' he exclaimed. 'I've just the job for you.'

'A job?' asked the giraffe. 'For me?'

'Yes,' said Mr Noah. 'Now that the rain has stopped you can act as our look-out for the first sight of land.'

'Can I?' asked the giraffe eagerly. 'Can I really?'

'Yes, please,' said Mr Noah.

So the giraffe stuck his long neck out of the trap at the top of the ark and looked for the first sight of land, while Mr Noah went to his cabin.

'Thank you, God,' he said. 'You said the rain would stop on the fortieth day and you said that there would be a job for the giraffe.'

And God looked down at the small ark floating under a cloudless sky, with the giraffe's head poking happily out of the top, and smiled.

10
THE JACKDAW'S TALE

When Mr Noah and his family arrived on the ark they brought little with them, other than the clothes they were wearing. God had told Mr Noah there would not be room for many possessions. His wife had carried a few precious pots and pans and wore her best robe, feeling that there was no point leaving it to be ruined in the flood. Her sons' wives had done the same.

But Miriam had brought some jewellery with her. A necklace of sparkling stones, which had been a present from her husband, Ham, and two brightly shining bracelets which had been given to her at her wedding.

'They don't take up any room at all,' she said to Ham, 'and it seems a shame to leave them behind.'

She wore them as she came aboard the ark, but afterwards put them at the back of a shelf in her cabin and forgot all about them. There was too much to do to think about wearing fine clothes or pretty jewellery.

But the jackdaw, who had seen Miriam wearing her

necklace and bracelets on that first day, could not forget
about them. He wanted them. He wanted them very
much indeed. He loved bright objects.

'It was the way they shone,' he told his wife. 'The
stones of the necklace were deep blue and white, just like
a cascade of water. And the bracelets... polished until
you could see your beak reflected in them.'

He could not eat, he could not sleep, and he talked
about them so much that at last his wife said, exasperated,

'Well, if you want to see them so much, why don't
you ask Miriam if you can look at them? I'm sure she
wouldn't mind.'

But the jackdaw wanted more than just one look. He
wanted them for himself. So he hung around Miriam's
cabin, keeping well into the shadows, and watched and
waited.

One evening he was rewarded. Miriam had gone out

leaving her cupboard door open. The jackdaw saw something shining at the back of a shelf and gently pulled out the necklace and the two bracelets and laid them in a glittering heap. Then he perched on the edge of the bed and gloated. They were lovely. Perfect.

Hearing a sound, he hurriedly snatched up a handkerchief, wrapped it round the jewellery, and flew off, carrying the bundle in his beak. He flew to a spot he had already thought would make a good hiding place and hid the bundle.

During the weeks that followed, the jackdaw never went to look at the jewellery he had stolen. It was too dangerous, he thought, and besides, there was no need. It would be safe where he had hidden it and would keep until the voyage was over and he could take it away from prying eyes and enjoy it in private.

Miriam did not miss her jewellery until the evening of the party. The elephants had organized the event in order to celebrate the end of the rain and Mrs Noah, Hannah, Rachel and she dressed for the occasion in their best robes.

'I know,' she said to Ham. 'I'll wear my necklace and my bracelets. I haven't worn them for ages and they'd look nice with this robe.'

She rummaged in the drawer.

'They're not here,' she said.

She looked again.

'They've gone!'

She said nothing about it during the party, for she did not wish to spoil the fun, but afterwards she and Ham searched right through their cabin. She asked Rachel and Hannah if they seen them, and then went to Mr and Mrs Noah.

'I know God told us not to bring many possessions,' she explained, 'but they weren't large and meant a great deal to me. I'd be very sorry to lose them.'

'I should think so, too,' said Mrs Noah comfortably. 'Noah, whatever can have happened to them?'

'I don't know,' said Mr Noah. 'Perhaps the animals have seen them. I'll ask.'

But when he called the animals together, no one admitted seeing the missing bracelets or the necklace.

'Just like humans to go losing things,' croaked the raven. 'Wouldn't find one of us doing it.'

'That's because we don't wear jewellery,' said the badger.

'We don't need to,' said the peacock, eyeing his newly-grown tail with satisfaction. 'We are altogether magnificent as we are.'

'Speak for yourself,' said the warthog. 'Some of us might look a bit better with some jewellery round our necks.'

'No amount of jewellery would make you look any better, old son,' said the fox, grinning.

'Nor you, foxy-face,' said the warthog amiably.

'Anyway,' said the goose. 'Why did Mr Noah allow her to bring her jewellery in the first place? It's not as if this was a pleasure cruise. It's a life and death voyage and I strongly disapprove of her bringing trinkets on board. *We* weren't allowed to bring anything.'

'That's because we haven't got anything *to* bring,' said the buffalo. 'Don't be such a misery. She's a pretty girl and the jewellery doesn't take up any room.'

'But where's it gone? That's what I want to know,' said the lion.

'Perhaps one of the other humans stole it,' said the woodpecker. 'I wouldn't put it past Shem's wife. She could do with a bit of jewellery to brighten herself up.'

The parrot laughed at that, but the lion frowned.

'This is a serious matter which affects us all,' he said. 'I'm ashamed to think of it happening on *my* ship. And I don't for one moment think we've heard the last of it.'

He was right. Mr Noah organized a search of the ark. Everyone joined in, even the jackdaw, but the missing jewellery was not to be found.

'It's a proper mystery,' Mr Noah said as he told God about it. 'I know it must seem very unimportant to you, God,' he added humbly. 'But it's important to Miriam, and I'm fond of the child and don't like to see her upset.'

'Everything is important to me, Noah,' God replied.

'We must have a thief on board,' Mr Noah said

unhappily. 'Whatever shall I do about it?'

'Do nothing,' said God. 'I have the matter in hand. Just be patient.'

But it was hard for Mr Noah to be patient, for every day his sons and their wives pestered him about the matter.

'It's in God's hands,' he told them.

'Well if it's in God's hands, why doesn't God give it back?' bleated the goat, who overheard this. 'And I really can't think why God wants two bracelets and a necklace anyway. When would he wear them?'

'Oh, don't be so silly,' snapped the fox.

Everyone was short-tempered just then.

'It's bad enough being stuck here now the rain's stopped,' muttered the otter. 'It's worse being under suspicion of theft as well. I'm that fed up!'

'We're only stuck here because everywhere is flooded,' explained the eagle. 'Once the water has gone down we can get off.'

'It's all right for you birds,' growled the otter.

It *was* all right for the birds. Every day they left the ark, flying further and further afield to exercise their wings, and for the sheer joy of being able to fly far into the sunlit sky. The jackdaw, however, never flew too far from the ark. He watched over his hiding place, afraid that it might be discovered, anxious for a glimpse of his spoils.

'Soon,' he thought. 'Soon, I'll be able to fly away and take the jewellery with me.'

His thoughts were interrupted. The giraffe, who had been on the look-out for the first sight of land, began to shout.

'Land ahoy,' he called excitedly. 'Land!'

There was a stampede for the roof.

'Be careful now!' Mr Noah shouted. 'We don't want anyone falling off!'

He tripped over his robe in his excitement as he climbed the stairs leading to the trapdoor in the roof of the ark.

'Where is it?' he asked the giraffe.

The giraffe pointed with his long neck. 'Over there.'

Mr Noah looked, then looked again. There was a dark shape on the horizon which could have been land . . .

. . . until it did a somersault and swam away, spouting a stream of water through its blowhole.

'I'm afraid it's just a whale,' Mr Noah said regretfully.

The animals began to make their way, rather dejectedly, down the stairs.

'Stop shoving!' said the penguin crossly.

'I wasn't,' said the deer.

'Yes, you were,' said the penguin. 'You shoved me in the back with your antler!'

'I didn't!' insisted the deer.

The penguin turned. Pushed into the space behind one of the stairs was a tattered piece of cloth covering something which jutted out sharply. The vibration of the animals as they thundered up to the roof had dislodged the bundle from its hiding place.

'Mr Noah!' called the penguin. 'I think I've found something.'

Mr Noah took the bundle into the great hall. Animals, insects and birds crowded round. Slowly he unwrapped it and brought out ... one necklace and two bracelets.

But they no longer shimmered and sparkled as they had done when they had last been worn by Miriam. They were now tarnished and dull, and covered in green mould.

The jackdaw and Miriam both cried out at the same time. Mr Noah turned to the jackdaw.

'Did you take Miriam's jewellery?' he asked.

The jackdaw hung his head. 'Well, I suppose ... in a manner of speaking ...'

'Yes or no?'

'Well ... yes ...'

'Why?'

'They sparkled so much,' said the jackdaw. 'They were so beautiful. I can't resist things that sparkle.'

'Stealing is very wrong,' Mr Noah said, shaking his head.

'I don't see why,' said the jackdaw. 'She shouldn't have brought them here in the first place. Putting temptation in my way.'

'That's no excuse,' said Mr Noah sternly. 'You know how upset Miriam has been and how everyone here has been under suspicion. It was a very bad thing to do.' He looked at the faded and dull objects in front of him. 'You stole them because they sparkled. I don't suppose you'd steal them now, would you?'

'No,' muttered the jackdaw. 'They're not beautiful any more.'

'What's happened to them?' asked the guinea-pig.

'The damp air has dulled them,' sighed Mr Noah. 'It's such a shame.'

Miriam burst into tears. 'They're ruined,' she said. 'My lovely necklace and my bracelets. All ruined.'

The jackdaw looked at Miriam's tear-stained face and felt ashamed.

'I didn't mean to upset you,' he said uncomfortably. 'I only thought how much *I* wanted them. I never thought about you at all.'

'How very selfish,' said the lion.

'Yes,' said the jackdaw. 'That's true. It was very wrong and very selfish.' He turned to Miriam. 'I'll try and make amends,' he said. 'If I clean them, do you think you could forgive me?'

Miriam sniffed. 'All right,' she said.

The jackdaw set to work and cleaned them so well that the necklace and the two bracelets shone brighter than before. Miriam was delighted and she put them on. The blue stones of the necklace reflected the deep blue of the sky and the white stones the fluffy white clouds that floated past. The bracelets sparkled and gleamed in the light from the sun. And the sun sparkled and gleamed on the water of the flood—as it began to dry up.

11

THE SNAKE'S TALE

Once the rain had stopped, Mr Noah and the animals, insects and birds on the ark kept a constant watch for the first sight of land. Many of the animals took to spending at least some part of each day up on the roof, especially as the weather was fine and sunny. The birds circled overhead and Mr Noah sent the dove away to look for a sign that the flood water was subsiding. When she returned with the leaf of an olive tree in her beak there was tremendous excitement.

'This means that the tree-tops are now above the water,' said Mr Noah with a broad smile.

The doves left the ark and did not return, and the exitement grew to fever pitch, although, as Mr Noah said, 'It will take time for dry land to appear.'

The animals now jostled one another for a place on the roof. Those with the keenest sight argued with one another as to who would be the first to sight land and the birds flew out each day, travelling great distances in their search.

But it was not an animal with good eyesight who first spotted land. Neither was it a bird. It was, rather surprisingly, the snake.

No one on board the ark liked the snakes very much.

'Scheming,' said the emu whenever she saw one or other of them.

'You never know where you are with a snake,' said the bear bluntly, and the larger animals agreed with him. The smaller animals were just scared.

'My dears, I simply *shudder* every time I see that snake looking at me with those *beady* eyes,' said the shrew dramatically. 'And that nasty, slimy skin. It gives me the creeps!'

'But we do have an agreement,' said the dormouse earnestly. 'Mr Noah made a rule that none of us is to be eaten on the ark.'

'Well *you* might have agreed to it and *I* might have agreed to it, but I doubt very much whether those snakes agreed to anything of the sort,' said the shrew. 'And as for *rules* . . . I wouldn't put it past the snakes to slither their way round rules if it suited them.'

Even Mr Noah, who tried to be fair to all the animals in his charge, could not repress a slight shudder when he saw a snake slithering down one of the wooden columns in the great hall or gliding noiselessly across the floor.

'I know they're part of your creation,' he said to God.

'But I can't like them. Those snakes have nasty, slippery ways.'

The snakes knew the feeling against them. It did not worry the snake's wife, but it bothered the snake.

'It's not as if we've done anything wrong,' he said fretfully. 'We've always been civil to the other animals whenever we've met.'

'Snakes have never been liked,' his wife said comfortably. 'I heard Mr Noah talking to his wife the other day about something that happened simply ages ago that involved a snake.'

'What was it?'

'I didn't hear all of it, but it seemed to be about two humans who lived in a beautiful garden in a place called Eden. Apparently God told them they could eat anything there, apart from the fruit of one particular tree.'

'What happened?' the snake asked.

'Well, they say that some ancestor of ours dared one of the humans to eat an apple from that tree, and she did.' The snake's wife paused. 'And no good came of it.'

'I should think not,' said the snake shuddering. 'Apples indeed! I'd choke if I ate an apple—and so would you.'

'I don't know if they choked,' said the snake's wife. 'I never heard the end of the story. But it seemed a bit unfair to blame the snake,' she added thoughtfully.

'And why take it out on us now?' asked the snake.

'We're not responsible for the things that happened in the past.'

'Everyone likes to have someone else to blame,' said his wife. 'It's only natural. So what if no one likes us?' She twisted herself into a complicated knot. 'I shouldn't let it worry you.'

But the snake did worry. He tried making friends with some of the animals, and even went so far as to perform in public, shedding his skin in one complete piece at the elephants' party. Everyone applauded at the time, but no one seemed to like him or his wife any better afterwards.

Once the weather improved, the snakes spent a lot of time on the roof, coiling themselves around one of the wooden supports to make sure that they did not slide off into the water.

'Move over there,' said the aardvark crossly. 'You're always up here, hogging the best places.'

'I don't know why you come up here anyway,' said the emu with a sniff. 'You won't be the first to see land. You're too low down.'

The snakes did not reply.

'And unimportant,' added the llama with a superior stare.

'I expect,' said the lion, 'that *I* shall see land first. After all, I am assistant to Mr Noah.'

'Or I shall,' said the eagle. 'I have wonderful eyesight.'

'At all events, it won't be you snakes,' said the aardvark. 'Now shift yourselves!'

The snakes obediently slithered to one side.

As mealtime approached the animals began to leave.

'Do you want to go down for some food?' asked the snake's wife.

'No,' said the snake. 'I'm not hungry.'

So they stayed where they were, the snake's wife half-asleep in the warm, still air, the snake wondering yet again just what he had done to make the animals dislike him so.

And then he saw it.

'Look,' he said to his wife. 'Out there. Do you see it?'

His wife lifted her head.

Far away on the horizon something dark and solid poked out of the water.

The snake uncoiled himself. 'I'm going to tell Mr Noah.'

He found Mr Noah serving food in the great hall.

'Mr Noah,' he hissed, leaning over his shoulder.

Mr Noah started and dropped the dish he was holding. 'Must you frighten me like that?' he said irritably.

'I'm so sorry,' said the snake. 'But I thought you ought to know that my wife and I have seen something.'

'What?' asked Mr Noah, still annoyed.

'It could be land,' said the snake, 'or it could be a large fish. We think you should come and look.'

'Land?' exclaimed the dingo. 'Did someone say— LAND?'

That did it. The meal forgotten, the animals rushed to the roof of the ark. The birds flew out in a great cloud and winged their way over to the dark shape, clearly visible on the horizon.

The eagle was the first to return.

'It *is* land,' he said in his great voice. 'The topmost peak of a mountain.'

'There!' said the lion crossly. '*I* should have been the one to have spotted it first!'

It was exciting news, but there was little anyone could do except watch as the ark slowly drifted towards the land.

'Say, doesn't anyone have any oars around here?' asked the pig loudly. 'It would make us go a bit quicker. I mean, this is a boat after all.'

'No,' said Mr Noah, 'God never told me to make any oars.'

'Well it must have been an oversight,' said the pig. 'A boat without oars is like . . .' he thought for a moment, ' . . . is like a sty without food,' he finished.

'What the ark needs is a good strong pair of flippers,' said the penguin seriously.

As the ark drew closer to land, the animals could see a strange shape on the summit, black and twisted against the sky.

'Whatever's that?' asked the dormouse.

The eagle flew across.

'How very sad,' he said on his return. 'It's the remains of a tree.'

'What's sad about that?' asked the beaver.

'It's dead,' said the eagle.

That silenced everyone and they all sat quietly watching as the speck of land grew steadily bigger. Then a stiff wind arose, whipping the water into steep white-crested waves. The small ark was tossed from side to side.

'Look!' said the eagle suddenly. 'The wind is driving the ark away!'

It was true. The ark was slowly being forced away from the land and out to sea.

'We must stop it at once,' said the beaver.

'How?' asked the fox.

'Well...' said the beaver. 'We should put down an anchor.'

Everyone turned to Mr Noah.

'I'm sorry,' he said unhappily, 'but God never mentioned an anchor.'

'Hmm,' said the monkey sourly. 'Doesn't surprise *me* in the least.'

'If I'd know how ill-equipped this vessel was, I'd never have come,' said the goat.

'Then you'd have drowned,' snapped the fox.

The beaver was peering ahead. 'Do we have any rope?' he asked. 'If we have, we could try to throw it round the stump of that tree.'

Everyone again turned to Mr Noah, who shook his head dumbly.

'I suppose... there's nothing you can do?' the dormouse asked Mr Noah anxiously.

'I can talk to God,' Mr Noah said, and that was what he did.

'I'm sure this is all part of your plan, God,' he said, a little doubtfully. The lack of oars, anchor and even rope had slightly dented his faith. 'But is there *anything* that can be done?'

'Have a little more faith, Noah,' said God bracingly. 'There's always something that can be done.'

Just at that moment the snake uncoiled himself from the wooden support.

'Come along, dear,' he said to his wife. 'I think we're needed.'

'You?' said the emu scornfully. 'What can *you* do?'

'We have our uses,' said the snake with dignity.

He knotted the end of his tail together with the end of his wife's tail.

'Are you ready?' he asked.

She nodded and grasped the wooden support firmly.

The snake coiled himself into a neat pile, took a deep breath, and threw himself off the roof. The animals gasped.

'Whatever's he doing?' asked the beaver.

The snake uncoiled in mid-air. He touched the tree with his forked tongue, but the tug of the ark dragged him back into the water. His wife hurriedly wrapped herself around the wooden support and pulled him back on board.

For a second time the snake threw himself towards the land. This time he caught hold of the tree, but a huge wave caused the ark to roll. The snake was dragged back once again.

'Third time lucky,' he said breathlessly. This time he was successful. He sank his fangs deep into the bark and held on tightly. The wind blew, the waves tugged, but the snake slowly coiled himself round the tree, hauling the ark in to land.

There was a rasping, grinding noise and the ark

slowly came to rest. The snake released his hold and came slithering, sliding back onto the boat, assisted by many hands.

'And do you know,' the shrew said afterwards to the dormouse. 'When I touched the snake I was *amazed*! It was the strangest thing, my dear, for that snake felt *perfectly* dry and quite warm—and we all know that snakes are nasty, slimy creatures. Now whatever do you make of that?'

'That we shouldn't judge by appearances,' the dormouse said dryly.

'No, indeed,' said the shrew. '*I* never do!'

Late that night, when all the celebrations were over, and the two snakes were wearily going towards their beds, they were stopped by Mr Noah.

'I've an apology to make,' he said. 'To you and to God.'

'Think nothing of it,' said the snake.

'What you did today has taught us all a lesson,' said Mr Noah.

'It won't last,' said the snake's wife. 'This will soon be forgotten, while that unfortunate ancestor of ours in the Garden of Eden will be remembered.' She looked at him and smiled a little sourly. 'We all like to think the worst of each other.' she said.

'Well, I'll never forget,' said Mr Noah.

And he never did.

12
THE RABBIT'S TALE

The ark had come to rest on the top of a mountain called Ararat and the flood water was subsiding. Every day a little more dry land could be seen and, at last, Mr Noah told the animals, insects and birds that they could leave the ark the following day.

'About time too,' said the panther, pacing restlessly up and down the great hall.

'Well, I can't say I'll be sorry to go,' said the fox. 'Although I must admit, it's been an experience.'

'One I could have done without,' muttered the monkey.

'Oh, I don't know,' said the donkey. 'Just think of all the different animals we've met. Ones I never knew existed.'

'And hope I never meet again,' the monkey added.

'We've been saved from the flood,' said the elephant. 'And I'm sure I never thought we would be.'

'It's due to Mr Noah,' said the beaver. 'He brought us safely through all the dangers.'

The lion coughed. 'With help and guidance from others,' he said.

'You mean God?' asked the beaver.

'Oh him, of course,' said the lion. 'But I meant, help from other *animals*.'

'Like you?' said the squirrel.

'Well . . . yes . . .' the lion agreed.

'And . . .?' added the tiger, a dangerous sparkle in his eye.

'And the tiger, of course,' the lion went on hurriedly. 'As Mr Noah's assistants, we have helped save every animal . . .'

' . . . *two* of every animal . . .' the tiger put in.

' . . . *two* of every animal, insect and bird in creation,' the lion continued. 'I think we might congratulate ourselves.'

'No one could accuse either of you of modesty,' the fox said sweetly.

'No,' said the lion complacently. 'I don't think anyone could.'

The tiger, who knew what the word meant, laughed.

'Didn't God have a hand in it somewhere?' the donkey asked mildly.

'Oh, he made the rules, of course,' the lion agreed. 'Two of every animal to enter the ark and two of every animal to leave it. Not one more and not one less. That's what he said and that's what we've done.'

The tiger nodded. 'One must always obey the rules.'

The rabbits, who had been listening to this conversation, looked at one another and went off to their burrow rather thoughtfully.

'What are we going to do?' the rabbit asked his wife.

'About...?'

'Yes, about...'

They looked down at the tiny new-born baby rabbit at their feet.

'Mr Noah won't mind,' said the rabbit's wife a little doubtfully.

'Maybe not, but God might,' said the rabbit. 'After all, you heard the lion.'

'If we don't tell Mr Noah then God won't know,' the rabbit's wife suggested.

'Yes, but how do we get the baby off the ark without Mr Noah finding out?' asked the rabbit.

His wife thought about it. 'I think we should speak to the lion. After all, he is Mr Noah's assistant.'

So the rabbits went to see the lion.

'We've a bit of a problem,' said the rabbit. 'And we wondered whether you could help us.'

'Of course,' said the lion graciously.

'You told us that God wanted two of every animal to enter the ark in order to be saved. That's right, isn't it?'

'Yes,' said the lion cautiously.

'And two of every animal were to leave the ark once

the flood had gone down. That was what you said, wasn't it?'

'Yes,' the lion agreed.

'Well the problem is, there aren't two rabbits on board. There are three, and we don't know what to do about it.'

'Hmm.' The lion thought for a moment. 'Have you spoken to Mr Noah?'

'Well no, not yet. You see we don't think *he* would mind, but he would tell God, and God might not be too happy about it,' said the rabbit's wife.

'God might not like his rules being changed,' the rabbit explained.

'Hmm,' said the lion again. 'A difficult one.' He was silent for a long time. 'I think I had better consult my colleague, the tiger,' he said at last, and padded off.

The tiger had no doubts at all.

'Rules are rules,' he said definitely, 'and not to be broken. Especially ones made by God. Two of every animal, insect and bird came on to the ark and two of every animal, insect and bird are to leave the ark—on the appointed day and at the appointed time.'

The eagle objected. 'But the two doves have already left,' he said.

'That's as maybe,' said the tiger. 'But there were only two of them and not a whole flock.'

'There's not a whole flock of rabbits,' said the rabbit's

wife. 'Only three of us and he's the dearest little thing.'

'Is he now?' the elephant's wife said comfortably. 'How nice.'

'Well, I agree with the tiger,' said the scorpion. 'One or fifty, it doesn't make any difference. If it's a rule, we can't change it.'

'Rules are rules,' the tiger said again. 'When we came on board Mr Noah laid down rules about not fighting and not eating each other. And we all abided by them, didn't we?

'Yes,' said the fox sadly. 'Although it wasn't easy.'

'We kept them because if you've got rules you must obey them,' the tiger said. 'Otherwise there's just confusion.'

There was silence after he had spoken.

'Look at it this way,' the tiger went on. 'If Mr Noah hadn't laid down the rule about not eating one another, there wouldn't have been two of every animal, insect and bird left alive to leave the ark tomorrow, would there?'

'No,' shuddered the dormouse. 'There probably wouldn't have been one dormouse, let alone two.'

'That *would* have been a pity,' said the fox, licking his lips.

'There's some sense in the rule about not eating one another,' said the jackal slowly. 'And I can see the sense in saying only two of every animal were to *enter* the ark, because otherwise there wouldn't have been any room. But I can't see the sense in God saying only two can *leave* the ark.'

'Perhaps he wanted to draw a line somewhere,' suggested the donkey. 'Otherwise the world would be overrun with rabbits...'

'Or donkeys, heaven help us,' said the monkey sourly.

'Or donkeys,' agreed the donkey.

'Look, I didn't make the rules,' said the tiger. 'I only carry them out. If you've any complaint, go and see Mr Noah. But to my mind it's quite clear. Two rabbits came on the ark so only two can leave the ark.'

'I won't leave my baby behind,' said the rabbit's wife stubbornly.

'I'm sure Mr Noah or God will look after the baby if you leave him,' said the lion.

'I wouldn't let anyone else bring up *my* baby,' said the kangaroo's wife.

'And what does Mr Noah, or God for that matter, know about bringing up a baby rabbit?' the rabbit's wife retorted.

'You should have thought of that earlier,' growled the tiger.

The debate among the animals continued throughout the night, and the rabbits had an endless stream of visitors, some to give their opinions, some to offer advice, and some just to look at the baby.

The following morning Mr Noah, Mrs Noah, their sons and their sons' wives came to the great hall early. Mr Noah opened the big door to the ark that God himself had closed at the start of the journey and sunlight streamed in. Everyone cheered.

Mr Noah stood at the entrance and ticked off the animals, insects and birds from his long list.

'Iguanas... now then... H... I... Ah, here we are. I hope you enjoyed the journey. Goodbye and God bless you both.'

The kangaroos were next.

'K... Let me see... I... J... K... That's right. Goodbye to you both and God bless you.'

He looked for a moment at the suspiciously large bump inside the kangaroo's pouch, but said nothing.

The two rabbits were waiting nervously.

'Rabbits... L... M... N... O... P... Q... R...
Here we are. Right down the bottom of the page. Two
rabbits. Hope you enjoyed the voyage.' He looked up,
smiling. 'Oh, and congratulations. What are you going
to call the baby?'

The rabbits were dumbfounded.

'However did you know?' they asked.

Mr Noah's smile broadened.

'You can't fool God,' he said. 'He told me. Your baby
can come out of the kangaroo's pouch now.'

The kangaroo's wife slowly brought the baby rabbit
out of her pouch and handed him to his mother.

'Why ever didn't you come and talk to me?' Mr Noah asked.

'Because we knew you would tell God and we didn't want God to know that we were breaking his rule,' said the rabbit's wife. 'We were afraid he would have been angry and forbidden us to take our baby away.'

'Why should he have done that?' Mr Noah asked, mystified.

'Because the tiger said that God told you to take two of every animal on to the ark and make sure that only two were to leave it.'

'Because God doesn't want the world over-populated by donkeys,' added the donkey helpfully.

'Rabbits,' said the monkey in a long-suffering voice.

'Oh, was it?' asked the donkey.

'And it wasn't me, it was the lion,' said the tiger hurriedly. 'I never said that.'

'But you agreed to it,' said the lion sweetly.

'Well, rules are made to be kept,' said the tiger stubbornly. 'Especially God's rules.'

'Yes,' said Mr Noah. 'Rules are made to be kept, but, with God's help, we must use our judgment about how they are to be applied. God would never have forbidden you to take your baby away.' He smiled. 'Who would have looked after it—me or God?'

'Just what I said,' said the rabbit's wife.

Mr Noah turned to the lion and the tiger. 'And God

never said that only two of every animal, insect and bird were to leave the ark. He told me to bring out of the ark every living creature in order to fill the earth, and that's what I've done.'

He gazed at the animals, who were crowding the green grass in front of him, with pleasure and satisfaction.

'My dear friends,' he said. 'For you are my friends. What's important to remember is that God deals with us in all sorts of ways, but always with the kind of love he showed in saving us from the flood.'

'And that's how you've dealt with us, Mr Noah,' said the eagle, who was perched high in the branches of a tall tree. 'With love and care for our safety. We all owe *you* a debt we can never repay.'

The murmur of agreement among the animals, insects and birds grew to a roar.

Mr Noah's eyes were bright with unshed tears. 'I only did what God told me to do,' he said. 'God bless you. All of you.'

13
THE END ...
AND THE BEGINNING

Mr Noah stared at the ark, which lay on its side on the mountain. It looked battered and worn. Its wooden hulk was water-stained and the lower part was covered with barnacles.

The animals, insects and birds had long since gone and everywhere was quiet. The only sound was that of running water.

'It's like a dream,' said Japheth.

'Or a nightmare,' said Ham.

'No,' said Mr Noah. 'Not a nightmare.'

'Did you ever doubt we'd make it, Father?' asked Shem.

Mr Noah sighed. 'Yes. Often. But I was wrong. I doubted God, and I should never have done that.'

The sky darkened and it began to rain.

'Is the flood starting all over again?' asked his wife.

'I don't know,' Mr Noah said. 'Is it, God?'

'No,' said God. 'I shall never again destroy all living things by water. Look up, Noah.'

Mr Noah looked up at the sky. The clouds parted and the sun shone out, its brilliant light reflecting against the rain. Mr Noah gasped. Red, orange, yellow, green, blue, indigo and violet, the colours flamed in the perfect arc of a rainbow.

'This rainbow is my promise to you and to all who live after you,' God said. 'Whenever you see a rainbow in the sky it will remind you that I will never again send a flood to destroy the earth. You have my promise.'

'Thank you, God,' said Mr Noah, but he did not look any happier.

'Cheer up, Noah,' God said, 'for this is a new beginning.'

'Yes,' said Mr Noah. 'I know.' He sighed again. 'It's funny, God, but now it's all over I feel rather flat. I miss the animals. Silly, isn't it? I didn't want the job in the first place and didn't really enjoy it while it was happening, but now it's over and they've all gone ...'

'But they haven't gone,' said God. 'Look around you.'

Mr Noah looked around. The trees below him were full of birds, busy making their nests. The air, fresh and clear after the shower of rain, was suddenly alive with their cries. A monkey swung from branch to branch of a tree while a squirrel raced up its trunk. Insects scurried at his feet, and he caught a glimpse of a dormouse running

across the green grass. Frogs were croaking in a nearby
pool of water, while a beaver was busily building a dam
across one of the many streams. A fox slunk away into the
undergrowth and, in the distance, Mr Noah could see the
elephants having an evening bathe. Butterflies drowsily
sunned themselves on a nearby bush and a bee buzzed
lazily past his nose.

'You're right, God,' Mr Noah said, feeling happier.
'They haven't gone.'

'Where are we going to sleep tonight, Father?' asked
Japheth anxiously.

'And how are we going to live?' demanded Ham.

Mr Noah smiled. 'Don't worry,' he said. 'We'll sleep
in the ark tonight and tomorrow we'll begin to build a

126

new farm. We'll make a new vineyard.' He looked at his wife and smiled. 'Would you like a new vineyard, Becky?'

'Yes,' said his wife, and smiled back at him.

A large shape approached. It was the lion. Behind him were a number of other animals, insects and birds.

'Mr Noah,' the lion said, 'forgive me for troubling you. We've been holding a meeting and I—as King of the Jungle—have been given the task . . .'

'Oh, get on with it!' said the fox impatiently.

' . . . given the *pleasant* task of offering our services to help you build your new farm,' the lion went on. 'We felt . . .'

Mr Noah felt something rubbing against his legs and looked down to see the cat, purring softly.

'We're quite good at moving heavy objects,' the elephant's wife interrupted.

'And I'm an expert in wood,' said the beaver. 'You needn't have any fears that your new home will leak.'

'I'm good at carrying burdens,' said the donkey.

'So am I,' added the camel.

'We work tirelessly, said the ant. 'Although we can't carry much at a time,' he added.

'We'll plant your vineyards,' said the tiger.

'And I'll tell the time,' crowed the cock.

'I can tell jokes,' said the giraffe eagerly.

Mr Noah lifted up the cat and begin stroking him.

'If you like,' said the spider, 'I'll spin a few cobwebs

in the corners of your house.'

'I'll add a touch of beauty to your garden,' said the peacock graciously, unfurling his lovely tail.

'You're not much use doing anything else,' the rhinoceros said bluntly.

'We'll form a Committee,' said the tiger. 'And I'll be Works Manager.'

'Hmm...' The lion cleared his throat.

'Perhaps there should be *two* Works Managers,' said Mr Noah tactfully. He looked around. 'I don't know what to say. Thank you. Thank you all.'

It was late when everyone finally left. Mr Noah and his family settled themselves to sleep. It was a clear, warm night and the moon shed a soft light. An owl hooted and the bats flitted among the trees. Mr Noah looked up at the sky, which was studded with bright stars, and felt at peace.

'Thank you, God,' he said. 'With your help, everything is possible.'

Then he turned over contentedly, and went to sleep.